The Thing in the Upper Room

Ruskin Bond is known for his signature simplistic and witty writing style. He is the author of several bestselling short stories, novellas, collections, essays and children's books; and has contributed a number of poems and articles to various magazines and anthologies. At the age of twenty-three, he won the prestigious John Llewellyn Rhys Prize for his first novel, *The Room on the Roof*. He was also the recipient of the Padma Shri in 1999, Lifetime Achievement Award by the Delhi Government in 2012, and the Padma Bhushan in 2014.

Born in 1934, Ruskin Bond grew up in Jamnagar, Shimla, New Delhi and Dehradun. Apart from three years in the UK, he has spent all his life in India, and now lives in Landour, Mussoorie, with his adopted family.

The Thing in the Upper Room

Selected and Compiled by
RUSKIN BOND

RUPA

Published by
Rupa Publications India Pvt. Ltd 2019
7/16, Ansari Road, Daryaganj
New Delhi 110002

Sales centres:
Allahabad Bengaluru Chennai
Hyderabad Jaipur Kathmandu
Kolkata Mumbai

ISBN: 978-93-5333-488-8

First impression 2019

10 9 8 7 6 5 4 3 2 1

CONTENTS

INTRODUCTION

Human imagination is a wonderful thing, but it can truly run wild with ghost stories. I have always had a fondness for tales of horror and dark mysteries because even the slightest oddity is enough to stir up considerable interest in me. But I also find it to be a difficult genre to crack for a writer—to conjure up something new, original and terrifying each time. And this is a collection of exactly that—some truly haunting stories. I personally like the ones that go beyond the tapping on doors in the middle of the night or a sinister wailing of the wind. And that is why I have put together this collection that will do more than just send shivers down your spine when you read it.

There are stories by greats such as E. and H. Heron, W.H. Hodgson, F. Marion Crawford, John Eyton, Marc Connelly, Algernon Blackwood, Milward Kennedy, Arthur Morrison, Margery Allingham, and many others.

Let me just add that most of the stories in this collection are great short stories in their own right—beautifully crafted, stylish and written with a fluency and clarity that is rare in modern fiction. The fact that these are scary or entertaining adds to their readability; but you can enjoy them as literature too.

Ruskin Bond

THEY NEVER GET CAUGHT

Margery Allingham

The murder was planned carefully, patiently, and carried
out without any fuss. The only person who was really
disconcerted was the victim. The queen of crime writing
at her best...

'Millie dear, this does explain itself, doesn't it? Henry.'
Mr Henry Brownrigg signed his name on the back of
the little blue bill with a flourish. Then he set the scrap of
paper carefully in the exact centre of the imperfectly scoured
developing bath, and, leaving the offending utensil on the kitchen
table for his wife to find when she came in, he stalked back to
the shop, feeling that he had administered the rebuke surely
and at the same time gracefully.

In fifteen years Mr Brownrigg felt that he had mastered the
art of teaching his wife her job. Not that he had taught her.
That, Mr Brownrigg felt, with a woman of Millie's staggering
obtuseness was past praying for. But now, after long practice,
he could deliver the snub or administer the punishing word in
a way which would penetrate her placid dullness.

Within half an hour after she had returned from shopping

and before lunch was set upon the table, he knew the bath would be back in the dark-room, bright and pristine as when it was new, and nothing more would be said about it. Millie would be a little more ineffectually anxious to please at lunch, perhaps, but that was all.

Mr Brownrigg passed behind the counter and flicked a speck of dust off the dummy cartons of face-cream. It was 12.25 and a half. In four and a half minutes Phyllis Bell would leave her office further down the High Street, and in seven and a half minutes she would come in through that narrow, sunlit doorway to the cool, drug-scented shop.

On that patch of floor where the sunlight lay blue and yellow, since it had found its way in through the enormous glass vases in the window which were the emblem of his trade, she would stand and look at him, her blue eyes limpid and her small mouth pursed and adorable.

The chemist took up one of the ebony-backed hand mirrors exposed on the counter for sale and glanced at himself in it. He was not altogether a prepossessing person. Never a tall man, at forty-two his wide, stocky figure showed a definite tendency to become fleshy, but there was strength and virility in his thick shoulders, while his clean-shaven face and broad neck were short and bull-like and his lips were full.

Phyllis liked his eyes. They held her, she said, and most of the other young women who bought their cosmetics at the corner shop and chatted with Mr Brownrigg across the counter might have been inclined to agree with her.

Over-dark, round, hot eyes had Mr Brownrigg; not at all the sort of eyes for a little, plump, middle-aged chemist with a placid wife like Millie.

But Mr Brownrigg did not contemplate his own eyes. He smoothed his hair, wiped his lips, and then, realizing that Phyllis was almost due, he disappeared behind the dispensing desk. It was as well, he always thought, not to appear too eager.

He was watching the door, though, when she came in. He saw the flicker of her green skirt as she hesitated on the step and saw her half eager, half apprehensive expression as she glanced towards the counter.

He was glad she had not come in when a customer was there. Phyllis was different from any of the others whose little histories stretched back through the past fourteen years. When Phyllis was in the shop Mr Brownrigg found he was liable to make mistakes, liable to drop things and fluff the change.

He came out from his obscurity eager in spite of himself, and drew the little golden-haired girl sharply towards him over that part of the counter which was lowest and which he purposely kept uncluttered.

He kissed her and the sudden hungry force of the movement betrayed him utterly. He heard her quick intake of breath before she released herself and stepped back.

'You—you shouldn't,' she said, nervously tugging her hat back into position.

She was barely twenty, small and young looking for her years, with yellow hair and a pleasant, quiet style. Her blue eyes were frightened and a little disgusted now, as though she found herself caught up in an emotion which her instincts considered not quite nice.

Henry Brownrigg recognized the expression. He had seen it before in other eyes, but whereas on past occasions he had been able to be tolerantly amused and therefore comforting and glibly reassuring, in Phyllis it irritated and almost frightened him.

'Why not?' he demanded sharply, too sharply he knew immediately, and the blood rushed into his face.

Phyllis took a deep breath.

'I came to tell you,' she said jerkily, like a child saying its piece, 'I've been thinking things over. I can't go on with all this. You're married. I want to be married some day. I—I shan't come in again.'

'You haven't been talking to someone?' he demanded, suddenly cold.

'About you? Good heavens, no!'

Her vehemence was convincing, and because of that he shut his mind to its uncomplimentary inference and experienced only relief.

'You love me,' said Henry Brownrigg. 'I love you and you love me. You know that.'

He spoke without intentional histrionics, but adopted a curious monotone which, some actors have discovered, is one of the most convincing methods of conveying deep sincerity.

Phyllis nodded miserably and then seemed oddly embarrassed. Wistfully her eyes wandered to the sunlit street and back again.

'Goodbye,' she said huskily and fled.

He saw her speeding past the window, almost running.

For some time Henry Brownrigg remained looking down at the patch of blue sunlight where she had stood. Finally he raised his eyes and smiled with conscious wryness. She would come back. Tomorrow, or in a week, or in ten days perhaps, she would come back. But the obstacle, the insurmountable obstacle would arise again, in time it would defeat him and he would lose her.

Phyllis was different from the others. He would lose her. Unless that obstacle were removed.

Henry Brownrigg frowned.

There were other considerations too. The old, mottled ledger told those only too clearly.

If the obstacle were removed it would automatically wipe away those difficulties also, for was there not the insurance and that small income Millie's father had left so securely tied, as though the old man had divined his daughter would grow up a fool?

Mr Brownrigg's eyes rested upon the little drawer under the counter marked: 'Prescriptions: private.' It was locked and not even young Perry, his errand boy and general assistant, who poked his nose into most things, guessed that under the pile of slips within was a packet of letters scrawled in Phyllis's childish hand.

He turned away abruptly. His breath was hard to draw and he was trembling. The time had come.

Some months previously Henry Brownrigg had decided that he must become a widower before the end of the year, but the interview of the morning had convinced him that he must hurry.

At this moment Millie, her face still pink with shame at the recollection of the affair of the ill-washed bath, put her head round the inner door.

'Lunch is on the table, Henry,' she said, and added with that stupidity, which had annoyed him ever since it had ceased to please him, by making him feel superior. 'Well, you do look serious. Oh, Henry, you haven't made a mistake and given somebody a wrong bottle?'

'No, my dear Millie,' said her husband, surveying her coldly and speaking with heavy sarcasm. 'That is the peculiar sort of idiot mistake I have yet to make. I haven't reached my wife's level yet.'

And as he followed her uncomplaining figure to the little room behind the shop a word echoed rhythmically in the back of his mind and kept time with the beating of his heart. 'Hurry! Hurry! Hurry!'

♦

'Henry, dear,' said Millie Brownrigg, turning a troubled face towards her husband, 'why Doctor Crupiner? He's so expensive and so old.'

She was standing in front of the dressing-table in the big front bedroom above the shop, brushing her brown, grey streaked hair before she plaited it and coiled it round her head.

Henry Brownrigg, lying awake in his bed on the far side of the room, did not answer her.

Millie went on talking. She was used to Henry's silence. Henry was so clever. Most of his time was spent in thought.

'I've heard all sorts of odd things about Doctor Crupiner,' she remarked. 'They say he's so old he forgets. Why shouldn't we go to Mother's man? She swears by him.'

'Unfortunately for your mother she has your intelligence, without a man to look after her, poor woman,' said Henry Brownrigg.

Millie made no comment.

'Crupiner,' continued Henry Brownrigg, 'may not be much good as a general practitioner, but there is one subject on which he is a master. I want him to see you. I want to get you well, old dear.'

Millie's gentle, expressionless face flushed and her blue eyes looked moist and foolish in the mirror. Henry could see her reflection in the glass and he turned away. There were moments when, by her obvious gratitude for a kind word from him, Millie made him feel a certain distaste for his project. He wished to God she would go away and leave him his last few moments in bed to think of Phyllis in peace.

'You know, Henry,' said Mrs Brownrigg suddenly, 'I don't feel ill. Those things you're giving me are doing me good, I'm sure. I don't feel nearly so tired at the end of the day now. Can't you treat me yourself?'

The man in the bed stiffened. Any compunction he may have felt vanished and he became wary.

'Of course they're doing you good,' he said with the satisfaction of knowing that he was telling the truth up to a point, or at least of knowing that he was doing nothing reprehensible—yet.

'I don't believe in patent medicines as a rule, but Fender's pills are good. They're a well-known formula, and they certainly do pick one up. But I just want to make sure that you're organically sound. I don't like you getting breathless when you hurry, and the colour of your lips isn't good, you know.'

Plump, foolish Millie looked in the mirror and nervously ran her forefinger over her mouth.

Like many women of her age she had lost much of her colour, and there certainly was a faint, very faint, blue streak round the edge of her lips.

The Chemist was heavily reassuring.

'Nothing to worry about, I'm sure, but I think we'll go down and see Crupiner this evening,' he said, and added adroitly, 'we want to be on the safe side, don't we?'

Millie nodded, her mouth trembling.

'Yes, dear,' she said, and paused, adding afterwards in that insufferable way of hers, 'I suppose so.'

When she had gone downstairs to attend to breakfast Henry Brownrigg rose with his own last phrase still on his lips. He repeated it thoughtfully.

'The safe side.' That was right. The safe side. No ghastly hash of it for Henry Brownrigg.

Only fools made a hash of things. Only fools got caught. This was almost too easy. Millie was so simple-minded, so utterly unsuspecting.

By the end of the day Mr Brownrigg was nervy. The boy

Perry had reported innocently enough that he had seen young Hill in his new car going down Acacia Road at something over sixty, and had added casually that he had had the Bell girl with him. The youngest one. Phyllis. Did Mr Brownrigg remember her? She was rather pretty.

For a moment Henry Brownrigg was in terror lest the boy had discovered his secret and was wounding him maliciously. But, having convinced himself that this was not so, the fact and the sting remained.

Young Hill was handsome and a bachelor. Phyllis was young and impressionable. The Chemist imagined them pulling up in some shady copse outside the town, holding hands, perhaps even kissing, and the heart which could remain steady while Millie's stupid eyes met his anxiously as she spoke of her illness turned over painfully in Henry Brownrigg's side at the thought of that embrace.

'Hurry.' The word formed itself again in the back of his mind. Hurry...hurry.

Millie was breathless when they arrived at Doctor Crupiner's old-fashioned house. Henry had been self-absorbed and had walked very fast.

Doctor Crupiner saw them immediately. He was a vast, dusty old man. Privately Millie thought she would like to take a good stiff broom to him, and the picture the idea conjured in her mind was so ridiculous that she giggled nervously and Henry had to shake his head at her warningly.

She flushed painfully, and the old, stupid expression settled down over her face again.

Henry explained her symptoms to the doctor and Millie looked surprised and gratified at the anxiety he betrayed. Henry had evidently noticed her little wearinesses much more often than she had supposed.

When he had finished his recital of her small ills, none of them alarming in themselves but piling up in total to a rather terrifying sum of evidence, Doctor Crupiner turned his eyes, which were small and greasy, with red veins in their whites, on to Millie, and his old lips, which were mottled like Henry's ledger, moved for a fraction of a second before his voice came, wheezy and sepulchral.

'Well, madam,' he said, 'your husband here seems worried about you. Let's have a look at you.'

Millie trembled. She was getting breathless again from sheer apprehension. Once or twice lately it had occurred to her that the Fender's pills made her feel breathless, even while they bucked her up in other ways, but she had not liked to mention this to Henry.

Doctor Crupiner came close to her, breathing heavily through his nose in an effort of concentration. He thrust a stubby, unsteady finger into her eye socket, dragging down the skin so that he could peer short-sightedly at her eyeball. He thumped her half-heartedly on the back and felt the palms of her hands.

Mr Brownrigg, who watched all this somewhat meaningless ritual, his round eyes thoughtful and uneasy, suddenly took the doctor on one side, and the two men had a muttered conversation at the far end of the long room.

Millie could not help overhearing some of it, because Doctor Crupiner was deaf these days and Henry was anxious to make himself understood.

'Twenty years ago,' she heard. 'Very sudden.' And then, after a pause, the awful word 'hereditary'.

Millie's trembling fit increased in intensity and her broad, stupid face looked frightened. They were talking about her poor Papa. He had died very suddenly of heart disease.

Her own heart jumped painfully. So that was why Henry seemed so anxious.

Doctor Crupiner came back to her. She had to undo her dress and Doctor Crupiner listened to her heart with an ancient stethoscope. Millie, already trembling, began to breathe with difficulty as her alarm became unbearable.

At last the old man finished with her. He stared at her unwinkingly for some seconds and finally turned to Henry, and together they went back to the far end of the room.

Millie strained her ears and heard the old man's rumbling voice.

'A certain irregularity. Nothing very alarming. Bring her to see me again.'

Then there was a question from Henry which she could not catch, but afterwards, as the doctor seemed to be fumbling in his mind for a reply, the Chemist remarked in an ordinary tone: 'I've been giving her Fender's pills.'

'Fender's pills?' Doctor Crupiner echoed the words with relief. 'Excellent. Excellent. You chemists like patent medicines, I know, and I don't want to encourage you, but that's a well-known formula and will save you mixing up my prescription. Carry on with those for a while. Very good things; I often recommend them. Take them in moderation, of course.'

'Oh, of course,' said Henry. 'But do you think I'm doing right, Doctor?'

Millie looked pleased and startled at the earnestness of Henry's tone.

'Oh, without doubt, Mr Brownrigg, without doubt,' Doctor Crupiner repeated the words again as he came back to Millie. 'There, Mrs Brownrigg,' he said with spurious jollity, 'you take care of yourself and do what your husband says. Come to see me again in a week or so and you'll be as right as ninepence.

Off you go. Oh, but Mrs Brownrigg, no shocks, mind. No excitements. No little upsets. And don't over-tire yourself.'

He shook hands perfunctorily, and, while Henry was helping Millie to collect her things with a solicitude quite unusual in him, the old man took down a large, dusty book from the shelves.

Just before they left he peered at Henry over his spectacles.

'Those Fender's pills are quite a good idea,' he remarked in a tone quite different from his professional rumble. 'Just the things. They contain a small percentage of digitalin.'

♦

One of Mr Brownrigg's least attractive habits was his method of spending Saturday nights.

At half-past seven the patient but silently disapproving Millie would clear away the remains of the final meal of the day and place one glass and an unopened bottle of whisky and a siphon of soda on the green serge tablecloth.

This done, she would retire to the kitchen, wash up, and complete the week's ironing. She usually left this job until then, because it was a longish business, with frequent pauses for minor repairs to Henry's shirts and her own underclothing, and she knew she had plenty of undisturbed time on her hands.

She had, in fact, until midnight. When the kitchen clock wheezed twelve, Millie folded her ironing board and turned up the irons on the stove to cool.

The she went into the living-room and took away the glass and the empty bottle, so that the daily help should not see them in the morning. She also picked up the papers and straightened the room.

Finally, when the gas fire had been extinguished, she attended to Henry.

A fortnight and three days after her first visit to Doctor Crupiner—the Doctor, at Henry's suggestion, had increased her dose of Fender's pills from three to five a day—she went through her Saturday ritual as usual.

For a man engaged in Mr Brownrigg's particular programme to get hopelessly and incapably drunk once, much less once a week, might well have been suicidal lunacy.

One small glass of whisky reduced him to taciturnity. Twelve large glasses of whisky, or one bottle, made of him a limp, silent sack of humanity, incapable of movement or speech, but, quite remarkably, not a senseless creature.

It might well have occurred to Millie to wonder why her husband should choose to transform himself into a Therese Raquin paralytic once every week in his life, but in spite of her awful stupidity she was a tolerant woman and honestly believed that men were odd, privileged creatures who took delight in strange perversions. So she humoured him and kept his weakness secret even from her mother.

Oddly enough, Henry Brownrigg enjoyed his periodical orgy. He did not drink during the week, and his Saturday experience was at once an adventure and a habit. At the outset of his present project he had thought of foregoing it until his plan was completed, but he realized the absolute necessity of adhering rigidly to his normal course of life, so that there could be no hook, however small, on which the garment of suspicion could catch and take hold.

On this particular evening Millie quite exhausted herself getting him upstairs and into bed. She was so tired when it was all over that she sat on the edge of her couch and breathed hard, quite unable to pull herself together sufficiently to undress.

So exhausted was she that she forgot to take the two Fender's pills that Henry had left on the dressing-table for her, and once in bed she could not persuade herself to get out again for them.

In the morning Henry found them still in the little box. He listened to her startled explanations in silence and then, as she added apology to apology, suddenly became himself again.

'Dear Millie,' he said in the old exasperated tone she knew so well, 'isn't it enough for me to do all I can to get you well without you hampering me at every turn?'

Millie bent low over the stove and, as if he felt she might be hiding sudden tears, his manner became more conciliatory.

'Don't you like them?' he inquired softly. 'Don't you like the taste of them? Perhaps they're too big? Look here, old dear, I'll put them up in an easier form. You shall have them in jelly cases. Leave it to me. There, there, don't worry. But you must take your medicine, you know.'

He patted her plump shoulder awkwardly and hurried upstairs to dress.

Millie became thoughtful. Henry was clearly very worried about her indeed, or he would never be so nice about her silly mistake.

◆

Young Bill Perry, Brownrigg's errand boy assistant, was at the awkward stage, if indeed he would ever grow out of it.

He was scrawny, red-headed, with a tendency to acne, and great raw, scarlet wrists. Mr Brownrigg he loathed as only the young can loathe the possessor of a sarcastic tongue, but Millie he liked, and his pale, sandy-fringed eyes twinkled kindly when she spoke to him.

Young Perry did not think Millie was half so daft as the Old Man made out.

If only because she was kind to him, young Perry was

interested in the state of Millie's health.

On the Monday night young Perry saw Mr Brownrigg putting up the contents of the Fender's pills in jelly cases and he inquired about them.

Mr Brownrigg was unusually communicative. He told young Perry in strict confidence that Mrs Brownrigg was far from well and that Doctor Crupiner was worried about her.

Mr Brownrigg also intimated that he and Doctor Crupiner were, as professional men, agreed that if complete freedom from care and Fender's pills could not save Mrs Brownrigg, nothing could.

'Do you mean she might die?' said young Perry, aghast. 'Suddenly, I mean, Sir?'

He was sorry as soon as he had spoken, because Mr Brownrigg's hand trembled so much that he dropped one of the jelly cases and young Perry realized that the Old Man was really wild about the Old Girl after all, and that his bullyragging her was all a sham to hide his feelings.

At that moment young Perry's sentimental, impressionable heart went out to Mr Brownrigg, and he generously forgave him for his observation that young Perry was patently cut out for the diplomatic service, since his tact and delicacy were so great.

The stores arrived. Bill Perry unpacked the two big cases; the smaller case he opened, but left the unpacking to his employer.

Mr Brownrigg finished his pill making, although he was keeping the boy waiting, rinsed his hands and got down to work with his usual deliberation.

There were not a great many packages in the case and young Perry, who had taken a peep at the mottled ledger some time before, thought he knew why. The Old Man was riding close to the edge. Bills and receipts had to be juggled very carefully these days.

The boy read the invoice from the wholesaler's, and Mr Brownrigg put the drugs away.

'Sodii Bicarbonas, Magnesia Levis,' he read, stumbling over the difficult words. 'Iodine, Quininae Hydrochloridum, Tincture Digitalin...that must be it, Mr Brownrigg. There, in the biggish packet.'

Bill Perry knew he read badly and was only trying to be helpful when he indicated the parcel, but Mr Brownrigg shot a truly terrifying glance in his direction as he literally snatched up the package and carried it off to the drug cabinet.

Young Perry was dismayed. He was late and he wanted to go. In his panic he floundered on, making matters worse.

'I'm sorry, sir,' he said. 'I was only trying to help. I thought you might be—er—thinking of something else and got a bit muddled.'

'Oh,' said Mr Brownrigg slowly, fixing him with those hot, round eyes in a way which was oddly disturbing. 'And of what should I be thinking when I am doing my work, boy?'

'Of—of Mrs Brownrigg, Sir,' stammered the wretched Perry helplessly.

Henry Brownrigg froze. The blood congealed in his face and his eyes seemed to sink into his head.

Young Perry, who realized he had said the wrong thing, and who had a natural delicacy which revolted at prying into another's sorrow, mistook his employer's symptoms for acute embarrassment.

'I'm sorry,' he said again. 'I was really trying to help. I'm a bit—er—windy myself, Sir. Mrs Brownrigg's been very kind to be. I'm sorry she's so ill.'

A great sigh escaped Henry Brownrigg.

'That's all right, my boy,' he said, with a gentleness his assistant had never before heard in his tone. 'I'm a bit rattled myself, too. You can go now. I'll see to these few things.'

Young Perry sped off, happy to be free on such a sunny evening, but also a little awe-stricken by the revelation of this tragedy of married love.

◆

Phylis hurried down Coe's Lane, which was a short cut between her own road and Priory Avenue. It was a narrow, paper-baggy little thoroughfare, with a dusty hedge on one side and a high tarred fence on the other.

On this occasion Coe's Lane appeared to be deserted, but when Phyllis reached the stunted may tree halfway down the hedge a figure stepped out and came to meet her.

The girl stopped abruptly in the middle of the path. Her cheeks were patched with pink and white and she caught her breath sharply as though afraid of herself.

Henry Brownrigg himself was unprepared for the savagery of the sudden pain in his breast when he saw her, and the writhing, vicious, mindless passion which checked his breathing and made his eyelids feel sticky and his mouth dry, frightened him a little also.

They were alone in the lane and he kissed her, putting into his hunched shoulders and greedy lips all the insufferable, senseless longing of the past eighteen days.

When he released her she was crying. The big, bright tears which filled her eyes brimmed over on to her cheeks and made her mouth look hot and wet and feverish.

'Go away,' she said and her tone was husky and imploring. 'Oh, go away—please, please!'

After the kiss Henry Brownrigg was human again and no longer the fiend-possessed soul in torment he had been while waiting in the lane. Now he could behave normally, for a time at least.

'All right,' he said, and added so lightly that she was deceived, 'going out with Peter Hill again this afternoon?'

The girl's lips trembled and her eyes were pleading.

'I'm trying to get free,' she said. 'Don't you see I'm trying to get free from you? It's not easy.'

Henry Brownrigg stared at her inquisitively for a full minute. Then he laughed shortly and explosively and strode away back down the lane at a great pace.

Henry Brownrigg went home. He walked very fast, his round eyes introspective but his step light and purposeful. His thoughts were pleasant. So Phyllis was there when he wanted her, there for the taking when the obstacle was once removed. That had been his only doubt. Now he was certain of it. The practical part of his project alone remained.

Small, relatively unimportant things like the new story the mottled ledger would have to tell when the insurance money was in the bank and Millie's small income was realized and reinvested crowded into his mind, but he brushed them aside impatiently. This afternoon he must be grimly practical. There was delicate work to do.

When he reached home Millie had gone over to her mother's.

It was also early-closing day and young Perry was far away, bowling wides for the St. Anne's parish cricket club.

Mr Brownrigg went round the house carefully and made sure that all the doors were locked. The shop shutters were up too, and he knew from careful observation that they permitted no light from within to escape.

He removed his jacket and donned his working overall, switched on the lights, locked the door between the shop and the living-room, and set to work.

He knew exactly what he had to do. Millie had been taking five Fender's pills regularly now for eight days. Each pill contained 1/16 gram Nativelle's Digitalin, and the stuff was cumulative. No wonder she had been complaining of biliousness and headaches lately! Millie was a hopeless fool.

He took out the bottle of Tincture Digitalin, which had come when young Perry had given him such a scare, and looked at it. He wished he had risked it and bought the Quevenne's, or the freshly powdered leaves. He wouldn't have had all this trouble now.

Still, he hadn't taken the chance, and on second thoughts he was glad. As it was, the wholesalers couldn't possibly notice anything unusual in his order. There could be no inquiry: it meant he need never worry—afterwards.

He worked feverishly as his thoughts raced on. He knew the dose. All that had been worked out months before when the idea had first occurred to him, and he had gone over this part of the proceedings again and again in his mind so that there could be no mistake, no slip.

Nine drachms of the tincture had killed a patient with no digitalin already in the system. But then the tincture was notoriously liable to deteriorate. Still, this stuff was fresh; barely six days old if the wholesalers could be trusted. He had thought of that.

He prepared his burner and the evaporator. It took a long time. Although he was so practised, his hands were unsteady and clumsy, and the irritant fumes got into his eyes.

Suddenly he discovered that it was nearly four o'clock. He was panic-stricken. Only two hours and Millie would come back, and there was a lot to be done.

As the burner did its work his mind moved rapidly. Digitalin was so difficult to trace afterwards; that was the beauty of it. Even the great Tardieu had been unable to state positively if it was digitalin that had been used in the Pommeraise case, and that after the most exhaustive P.M. and tests on frogs and all that sort of thing.

Henry Brownrigg's face split into the semblance of a smile. Old Crupiner was no Tardieu. Crupiner would not advise a P.M. if he could possibly avoid it. He'd give the certificate all right; his mind was prepared for it. Probably he wouldn't even come and look at the body.

Millie's stupid, placid body. Henry Brownrigg put the thought from him. No use getting nervy now.

A shattering peal on the back door startled him so much that he nearly upset his paraphernalia. For a moment he stood breathing wildly, like a trapped animal, but he pulled himself together in the end, and, changing into his coat, went down to answer the summons.

He locked the shop door behind him, smoothed his hair, and opened the back door confident that he looked normal, even ordinary.

But the small boy with the evening paper did not wait for his Saturday's sixpence but rushed away after a single glance at Mr Brownrigg's face. He was a timid twelve-year-old, however, who often imagined things, and his employer, an older boy, cuffed him for the story and made a mental note to call for the money himself on the Monday night.

The effect of the incident on Henry Brownrigg was considerable. He went back to his work like a man in a nightmare, and for the rest of the proceedings he kept his mind resolutely on the physical task.

At last it was done.

He turned out the burner, scoured the evaporator, measured

the toxic dose carefully, adding to it considerably to be on the safe side. After all, one could hardly overdo it; that was the charm of this stuff.

Then he effectively disposed of the residue and felt much better.

He had locked the door and changed his coat again before he noticed the awful thing. A layer of fine dust on the top of one of the bottles first attracted his attention. He removed it with fastidious care. He hated a frowsy shop.

He had replaced his handkerchief before he saw the showcase ledge and the first glimmering of the dreadful truth percolated his startled mind.

From the ledge his eyes travelled to the counter top, to the dummy cartoons, to the bottles and jars, to the window shutters, to the very floor.

Great drops appeared on Henry Brownrigg's forehead. There was not an inch of surface in the whole shop that was innocent of the thinnest, faintest coat of yellowish dust.

Digitalin! Digitalin over the whole shop! Digitalin over the whole world! The evidence of his guilt everywhere, damning, unescapable, clear to the first intelligent observer.

Henry Brownrigg stood very still.

Gradually his brain, cool at the bidding of the instinct of selfpreservation, began to work again. Delay. That was the all-important note. Millie must not take the capsule tonight as he had planned. Not tonight, nor tomorrow. Millie must not die until every trace of that yellow dust had been driven from the shop.

Swiftly he rearranged his plan. Tonight he must behave as usual and tomorrow, when Millie went to church, he must clear off the worst of the stuff before young Perry noticed anything.

Then on Monday he would make an excuse and have the

vacuum cleaning people in. They came with a great machine and put pipes in through the window. He had often said he would have it done.

They worked quickly; so on Tuesday...

Meanwhile, normality. That was the main thing. He must do nothing to alarm Millie or excite her curiosity.

It did not occur to him that there would be a grim irony in getting Millie to help him dust the shop that evening. But he dismissed the idea. They'd never do it thoroughly in time.

He washed in the kitchen and went back into the hall. A step on the stairs above him brought a scream to his throat which he only just succeeded in stifling.

It was Millie. She had come in the back way without him hearing her, heaven knew how long before.

'I've borrowed a portiere curtain from Mother for your bedroom door, Henry,' she said mildly. 'You won't be troubled by the draught up there any more. It's such a good thick one. I've just been fixing it up. It looks very nice.'

Henry Brownrigg made a noise which might have meant anything. His nerves had gone to pieces.

Her next remark was reassuring, however; so reassuring that he almost laughed aloud.

'Oh, Henry,' she said, 'you only gave me four of those pills today, dear. You won't forget the other one, will you?'

◆

'Cold ham from the cooked meat shop, cold tinned peas, potato salad and Worcester sauce. What a cook! What a cook I've married, my dear Millie.'

Henry Brownrigg derived a vicious pleasure from the clumsy sarcasm, and when Millie's pale face became wooden he was gratified.

As he sat at the small table and looked at her he was aware of a curious phenomenon. The woman stood out from the rest of the room's contents as though she alone was in relief. He saw every line of her features, every fold of her dark cotton foulard dress, as though they were drawn with a thick black pencil.

Millie was silent. Even her usual flow of banality had dried up, and he was glad of it.

He found himself regarding her dispassionately, as though she had been a stranger. He did not hate her, he decided. On the contrary, he was prepared to believe that she was quite an estimable, practicable person in her own limited fashion. But she was in the way.

This plump, fatuous creature, not even different in her very obtuseness from many of the other matrons in the town, had committed the crowning impudence of getting in the way of Henry Brownrigg. She, this ridiculous, lowly woman, actually stood between Henry Brownrigg and the inmost desires of his heart.

It was an insight into the state of the Chemist's mind that at that moment nothing impressed him so forcibly as her remarkable audacity.

Monday, he thought. Monday, and possibly Tuesday, and then... Millie cleared away.

Mr Brownrigg drank his first glass of whisky and soda with a relish he did not often experience. For him the pleasure of his Saturday night libations lay in the odd sensation he experienced when really drunk.

When Henry Brownrigg was a sack of limp, uninviting humanity to his wife and the rest of the world, to himself he was a quiet, all-powerful ghost, seated, comfortable and protected, in the shell of his body, able to see and comprehend everything, but too mighty and too important to direct any of the drivelling little matters which made up his immediate world.

On these occasions Henry Brownrigg tasted godhead.

The evening began like all the others, and by the time there was but an inch of amber elixir in the square bottle, Millie and the dust in the shop and Doctor Crupiner had become in his mind as ants and ant burdens, while he towered above them, a colossus in mind and power.

When the final inch had dwindled to a yellow stain in the bottom of the white glass bottle, Mr Brownrigg sat very still. In a few minutes now he would attain the peak of that ascendancy over his fellow mortals when the body, so important to them, was for him literally nothing; not even a dull encumbrance, not even a nerveless covering but a nothingness, an unimportant, unnoticed element.

When Millie came in at last a pin could have been thrust deep into Mr Brownrigg's flesh and he would not have noticed it.

It was when he was in bed, his useless body clad in clean pyjamas, that he noticed that Millie was not behaving quite as usual. She had folded his clothes neatly on the chair at the end of the bed when he saw her peering at something intently.

He followed her eyes and saw for the first time the new portiere curtain. It certainly was a fine affair, a great, thick, heavy plush thing that looked as though it would stop any draught there ever had been.

He remembered clearly losing his temper with Millie in front of young Perry one day, and, searching in his mind for a suitable excuse, had invented this draught beneath his bedroom door. And there wasn't one, his ghost remembered; that was the beauty of it. The door fitted tightly in the jamb. But it gave Millie something to worry about.

Millie went out of the room without extinguishing the

lights. He tried to call out to her and only then realized the disadvantage of being a disembodied spirit. He could not speak, of course.

He was lying puzzled at this obvious flaw in his omnipotence when he heard her go downstairs instead of crossing into her room. He was suddenly furious and would have risen, had it been possible. But in the midst of his anger he remembered something amusing and lay still, inwardly convulsed with secret laughter.

Soon Millie would be dead. Dead-dead-dead. Millie would be stupid no longer.

Millie would appal him by her awful mindlessness no more. Millie would be dead.

She came up again and stepped softly into the room.

The alcohol was beginning to take its full effect now and he could not move his head. Soon oblivion would come and he would leave his body and rush off into the exciting darkness, not to return until the dawn.

He saw only Millie's head and shoulders when she came into his line of vision. He was annoyed. She still had those thick black lines round her, and there was an absorbed expression upon her face which he remembered seeing before when she was engrossed in some particularly difficult household task.

She switched out the light and then went over to the far window. He was interested now, and saw her pull up the blinds.

Then to his astonishment he heard the crackle of paper; not an ordinary crackle, but something familiar, something he had heard hundreds of times before.

He placed it suddenly. Sticky paper. His own reel of sticky paper from the shop.

He was so cross with her for touching it that for some moments he did not wonder what she was doing with it, and it was not until he saw her silhouetted against the second row of panes that he guessed. She was sticking up the window cracks.

His ghost laughed again. The draught. Silly, stupid Millie trying to stop the draught.

She pulled down the blinds and turned on the light again. Her face was mild and expressionless as ever, her blue eyes vacant and foolish.

He saw her go to the dressing-table, still moving briskly, as she always did when working about the house.

Once again the phenomenon he had noticed at the evening meal became startlingly apparent. He saw her hand and its contents positively glowing because of its black outline, thrown up in high relief against the white table cover.

Millie was putting two pieces of paper there: one white with a deckle edge, one blue and familiar.

Henry Brownrigg's ghost yammered in its prison. His body ceased to be negligible: it became a coffin, a sealed, leaden coffin suffocating him in its senseless shell. He fought to free himself, to stir that mighty weight, to move.

Millie knew.

The white paper with the deckle edge was a letter from Phyllis out of the drawer in the shop, and the blue paper—he remembered it now—the blue paper he had left in the dirty developing bath.

He re-read his own pencilled words as clearly as if his eye had become possessed of telescopic sight:

'Millie dear, this does explain itself, doesn't it?'

And then his name, signed with a flourish. He had been so pleased with himself when he had written it.

He fought wildly. The coffin was made of glass now, thick, heavy glass which would not respond to his greatest effort.

Millie was hesitating. She had picked up Phyllis's letter.

Now she was reading it again.

He saw her frown and tear the paper into shreds, thrusting the pieces into the pocket of her cardigan.

Henry Brownrigg understood. Millie was sorry for Phyllis. For all her obtuseness she had guessed at some of the girl's piteous infatuation and had decided to keep her out of it.

What then? Henry Brownrigg writhed inside his inanimate body.

Millie was back at the table now. She was putting something else there. What was it? Oh, what was it?

The ledger! He saw it plainly, the old, mottled ledger, whose story was plain for any fool coroner to read and misunderstand.

Millie had turned away now. He hardly noticed her pause before the fireplace. She did not stoop. Her felt-shod slipper flipped the gas tap over.

Then she passed out of the door, extinguishing the light as she went. He heard the rustle of the thick curtain as she drew the wood close. There was an infinitesimal pause and then the key turned in the lock.

She had behaved throughout the whole proceeding as though she had been getting dinner or tidying the spare room.

In his prison Henry Brownrigg's impotent ghost listened. There was a hissing from the far end of the room.

In the attic, although he could not possibly hear it, he knew the metre ticked every two or three seconds.

Henry Brownrigg saw in a vision the scene in the morning. Every room in the house had the same key, so Millie would have no difficulty in explaining that on awakening she had noticed the smell of gas and, on finding her husband's door locked, had opened it with her own key.

The ghost stirred in its shell. Once again the earth and earthly incidents looked small and negligible. The oblivion was coming, the darkness was waiting; only now it was no longer exciting darkness.

The shell moved. He felt it writhe and choke. It was fighting—fighting—fighting.

The darkness drew him. He was no longer conscious of the shell now. It had been beaten. It had given up the fight.

The streak of light beneath the blind where the street lamp shone was fading. Fading. Now it was gone.

As Henry Brownrigg's ghost crept out into the cold, a whisper came to it, ghastly in its conviction:

'They never get caught, that kind. They're too dull, too practical, too unimaginative. They never get caught.'

THE STORY OF YAND MANOR HOUSE

E. and H. Heron

L ooking through the notes of Mr Flaxman Low, one sometimes catches through the steel-blue hardness of facts, the pink flush of romance, or more often the black corner of a horror unnameable. The following story may serve as an instance of the latter. Mr Low not only unravelled the mystery at Yand, but at the same time justified his life-work to M. Thierry, the well-known French critic and philosopher.

At the end of a long conversation, M. Thierry, arguing from his own standpoint as a materialist, had said:

'The factor in the human economy which you call "soul" cannot be placed.'

'I admit that,' replied Low. 'Yet, when a man dies, is there not one factor unaccounted for in the change that comes upon him? Yes? For though his body still exists, it rapidly falls to pieces, which proves that that has gone which held it together.'

The Frenchman laughed, and shifted his ground.

'Well, for my part, I don't believe in ghosts. Spirit manifestations, occult phenomena—is not this the ashbin into which a certain clique shoot everything they cannot understand, or for which they fail to account?'

'Then what should you say to me, Monsieur, if I told you that I have passed a good portion of my life in investigating this particular ashbin, and have been lucky enough to sort a small part of its contents with tolerable success?' replied Flaxman Low.

'The subject is doubtlessly interesting—but I should like to have some personal experience in the matter,' said Thierry dubiously.

'I am at present investigating a most singular case,' said Low. 'Have you a day or two to spare?'

Thierry thought for a minute or more.

'I am grateful,' he replied. 'But, forgive me, is it a convincing ghost?'

'Come with me to Yand and see. I have been there once already, and came away for the purpose of procuring information from MSS, to which I have the privilege of access, for I confess that the phenomena at Yand lie altogether outside any former experience of mine.'

Low sank back into his chair with his hands clasped behind his head—a favourite position of his—and the smoke of his long pipe curled up lazily into the golden face of an Isis, which stood behind him on a bracket. Thierry, glancing across, was struck by the strange likeness between the faces of the Egyptian goddess and this scientist of the nineteenth century. On both rested the calm, mysterious abstraction of some unfathomable thought. As he looked, he decided.

'I have three days to place at your disposal.'

'I thank you heartily,' replied Low. 'To be associated with so brilliant a logician as yourself in an inquiry of this nature is more than I could have hoped for! The material with which I have to deal is so elusive, the whole subject is wrapped in such obscurity and hampered by so much prejudice, that I can find few really qualified persons who care to approach these investigations seriously. I go down to Yand this evening, and hope not to leave without clearing up the mystery. You will accompany me?'

'Most certainly. Meanwhile, pray tell me something of the affair.'

'Briefly the story is as follows. Some weeks ago I went to Yand Manor House at the request of the owner, Sir George Blackburton, to see what I could make of the events which took place there. All they complain of is the impossibility of remaining in one room—the dining-room.'

'What then is he like, this M. le Spook?' asked the Frenchman, laughing.

'No one has ever seen him, or for that matter heard him.'

'Then how—'

'You can't see him, nor hear him, nor smell him,' went on Low, 'but you can feel him and—taste him!'

'*Mon Dieu!* But this is singular! Is he then of so bad a flavour?'

'You shall taste for yourself,' answered Flaxman Low, smiling. 'After a certain hour no one can remain in the room, they are simply crowded out.'

'But who crowds them out?' asked Thierry.

'That is just what I hope we may discover tonight or tomorrow.'

The last train that night dropped Mr Flaxman Low and his companion at a little station near Yand. It was late, but a trap in waiting soon carried them to the Manor House. The big bulk of the building stood up in absolute blackness before them.

'Blackburton was to have met us, but I suppose he has not yet arrived,' said Low. 'Hullo? The door is open,' he added as he stepped into the hall.

Beyond a dividing curtain they now perceived a light. Passing behind this curtain they found themselves at the end of the long hall, the wide staircase opening up in front of them.

'But who is this?' exclaimed Thierry.

Swaying and stumbling at every step, there tottered slowly down the stairs the figure of a man. He looked as if he had been drinking, his face was livid, and his eyes sunk into his head.

'Thank Heaven you've come! I heard you outside,' he said in a weak voice.

'It's Sir George Blackburton,' said Low, as the man lurched forward and pitched into his arms.

They laid him down on the rugs and tried to restore consciousness.

'He has the air of being drunk, but it is not so,' remarked Thierry. 'Monsieur has had a bad shock of the nerves. See the pulses drumming in his throat.'

In a few minutes Blackburton opened his eyes and staggered to his feet.

'Come. I could not remain there alone. Come quickly.'

They went rapidly across the hall, Blackburton leading the way down a wide passage to a double-leaved door, which, after a perceptible pause, he threw open, and they all entered together.

On the great table in the centre stood an extinguished lamp, some scattered food, and a big, lighted candle. But the eyes of all three men passed at once to a dark recess beside the heavy, carved chimneypiece, where a rigid shape sat perched on the back of a huge oak chair.

Flaxman Low snatched up the candle and crossed the room towards it.

On the top of the chair, with his feet upon the arms, sat a powerfully built young man huddled up. His mouth was open, and his eyes twisted upwards. Nothing further could be seen from below but the ghastly pallor of cheek and throat.

'Who is this?' cried Low. Then he laid his hand gently on the man's knee.

At the touch the figure collapsed in a heap upon the floor, the gaping, set, terrified face turned up to theirs.

'He's dead?' said Low after a hasty examination. 'I should say he's been dead some hours.'

'Oh, Lord! Poor Batty!' groaned Sir George, who was entirely unnerved. 'I'm glad you've come.'

'Who is he?' said Thierry, 'And what was he doing here?'

'He's a gamekeeper of mine. He was always anxious to try conclusions with the ghost, and last night he begged me to lock him in here with food for twenty-four hours. I refused at first, but then I thought if anything happened while he was in here alone, it would interest you. Who could imagine it would end like this?'

'When did you find him?' asked Low.

'I only got here from my mother's half an hour ago. I turned on the light in the hall and came in here with a candle. As I entered the room, the candle went out, and—and—I think I must be going mad.'

'Tell us everything you saw,' urged Low.

'You will think I am beside myself; but as the light went out and I sank almost paralysed into an armchair, I saw two barred eyes looking at me!'

'Barred eyes? What do you mean?'

'Eyes that looked at me through thin vertical bars, like the bars of a cage. What's that?'

With a smothered yell Sir George sprang back. He had approached the dead man and declared something had brushed his face.

'You were standing on this spot under the overmantel. I

will remain here. Meantime, my dear Thierry, I feel sure you will help Sir George to carry this poor fellow to some more suitable place,' said Flaxman Low.

When the dead body of the young gamekeeper had been carried out, Low passed slowly round and about the room. At length he stood under the old carved overmantel, which reached to the ceiling and projected bodily forward in quaint heads of satyrs and animals. One of these on the side nearest the recess represented a griffin with a flanged mouth. Sir George had been standing directly below this at the moment when he felt the touch on his face. Now alone in the dim, wide room, Flaxman Low stood on the same spot and waited. The candle threw its dull yellow rays on the shadows which seemed to gather closer and wait also. Presently a distant door banged, and Low, leaning forward to listen, distinctly felt something on the back of his neck!

He swung round. There was nothing! He searched carefully on all sides, then put his hand up to the griffin's head. Again came the same soft touch, this time upon his hand, as if something had floated past on the air.

This was definite. The griffin's head located it. Taking the candle to examine more closely, Low found four long black hairs depending from the jagged fangs. He was detaching them when Thierry reappeared.

'We must get Sir George away as soon as possible,' he said.

'Yes, we must take him away, I fear,' agreed Low. 'Our investigation must be put off till tomorrow.'

On the following day they returned to Yand. It was a large country-house, pretty and old-fashioned, with lattice windows and deep gables, that looked out between tall shrubs and across lawns set with beaupots, where peacocks sunned themselves on the velvet turf. The church spire peered over the trees on one side; and an old wall covered with ivy and creeping plants, and pierced at intervals with arches, alone separated the gardens from the churchyard.

The haunted room lay at the back of the house. It was square and handsome, and furnished in the style of the last century. The oak overmantel reached to the ceiling, and a wide window, which almost filled one side of the room, gave a view of the west door of the church.

Low stood for a moment at the open window looking out at the level sunlight which flooded the lawns and parterres.

'See that door sunk in the church wall to the left?' said Sir George's voice at his elbow. 'That is the door of the family vault. Cheerful outlook, isn't it?'

'I should like to walk across there presently,' remarked Low.

'What? Into the vault?' asked Sir George, with a harsh laugh. 'I'll take you if you like. Anything else I can show you or tell you?'

'Yes. Last night I found this hanging from the griffin's head,' said Low, producing the thin wisp of black hair. 'It must have touched your cheek as you stood below. Do you know to whom it can belong?'

'It's a woman's hair? No, the only woman who has been in this room to my knowledge for months is an old servant with grey hair, who cleans it,' returned Blackburton. 'I'm sure it was not here when I locked Batty in.'

'It is human hair, exceedingly coarse and long uncut,' said Low; 'but it is not necessarily a woman's.'

'It is not mine at any rate, for I'm sandy; and poor Batty was fair. Goodnight; I'll come round for you in the morning.'

Presently, when the night closed in, Thierry and Low settled down in the haunted room to await developments. They smoked and talked deep into the night. A big lamp burned brightly on the table, and the surroundings looked homely and desirable.

Thierry made a remark to that effect, adding that perhaps the ghost might see fit to omit his usual visit.

'Experience goes to prove that ghosts have a cunning habit of choosing persons either credulous or excitable to experiment upon,' he added.

To M. Thierry's surprise, Flaxman Low agreed with him.

'They certainly choose suitable persons,' he said, 'that is, not credulous persons, but those whose senses are sufficiently keen to detect the presence of a spirit. In my own investigations, I try to eliminate what you would call the supernatural element. I deal with these mysterious affairs as far as possible on material lines.'

'Then what do you say of Batty's death? He died of fright simply.'

'I hardly think so. The manner of his death agrees in a peculiar manner with what we know of the terrible history of this room. He died of fright and pressure combined. Did you hear the doctor's remark? It was significant. He said: "The indications are precisely those I have observed in persons who have been crushed and killed in a crowd!"'

'That is sufficiently curious, I allow. I see that it is already past two o'clock. I am thirsty; I will have a little seltzer.' Thierry rose from his chair, and, going to the sideboard, drew a tumblerful from the syphon. 'Pah! What an abominable taste!'

'What? The seltzer?'

'Not at all?' returned the Frenchman irritably. 'I have not touched it yet. Some horrible fly has flown into my mouth, I suppose. Pah! Disgusting!'

'What is it like?' asked Flaxman Low, who was at the moment wiping his own mouth with his handkerchief.

'Like? As if some repulsive fungus had burst in the mouth.'

'Exactly. I perceive it also. I hope you are about to be convinced.'

'What?' exclaimed Thierry, turning his big figure round and staring at Low. 'You don't mean—'

As he spoke the lamp suddenly went out.

'Why, then, have you put the lamp out at such a moment?' cried Thierry.

'I have not put it out. Light the candle beside you on the table.'

Low heard the Frenchman's grunt of satisfaction as he found the candle, then the scratch of a match. It sputtered and went out. Another match and another behaved in the same manner, while Thierry swore freely under his breath.

'Let me have your matches, Monsieur Flaxman; mine are, no doubt damp,' he said at last.

Low rose to feel his way across the room. The darkness was dense.

'It is the darkness of Egypt—it may be felt. Where then are you, my dear friend?' he heard Thierry saying, but the voice seemed a long way off.

'I am coming,' he answered, 'but it's so hard to get along.'

After Low had spoken the words, their meaning struck him. He paused and tried to realize in what part of the room he was. The silence was profound, and the growing sense of oppression seemed like a nightmare. Thierry's voice sounded again, faint and receding.

'I am suffocating, Monsieur Flaxman, where are you? I am near the door. Ach!'

A strangling bellow of pain and fear followed, that scarcely reached Low through the thickening atmosphere.

'Thierry, what is the matter with you?' he shouted. 'Open the door.'

But there was no answer. What had become of Thierry in that hideous, clogging gloom? Was he also dead, crushed in some ghastly fashion against the wall? What was this?

The air had become palpable to the touch, heavy, repulsive, with the sensation of cold humid flesh!

Low pushed out his hands with a mad longing to touch a table, a chair, anything but this clammy, swelling softness that thrust itself upon him from every side, baffling him and filling his grasp.

He knew now that he was absolutely alone—struggling against what?

His feet were slipping in his wild efforts to feel the floor—the dank flesh was creeping upon his neck, his cheek—his breath came short and labouring as the pressure swung him gently to and fro, helpless, nauseated?

The clammy flesh crowded upon him like the bulk of some fat, horrible creature; then came a stinging pain on the cheek. Low clutched at something—there was a crash and a rush of air—

The next sensation of which Mr Flaxman Low was conscious was one of deathly sickness. He was lying on wet grass, the wind blowing over him, and all the clean, wholesome smells of the open air in his nostrils.

He sat up and looked about him. Dawn was breaking windily in the east, and by its light he saw that he was on the lawn of Yand Manor House. The latticed window of the haunted room above him was open. He tried to remember what had happened. He took stock of himself, in fact, and slowly felt that he still held something clutched in his right hand—something dark-coloured, slender, and twisted. It might have been a long shred of bark or the cast skin of an adder—it was impossible to see in the dim light.

After an interval, the recollection of Thierry recurred to him. Scrambling to his feet, he raised himself to the window sill and looked in. Contrary to his expectation, there was no upsetting of furniture; everything remained in position as when the lamp went out. His own chair and the one Thierry had occupied were just as when they had arisen from them. But there was no sign of Thierry.

Low jumped in by the window. There was the tumbler full of seltzer, and the litter of matches about it. He took up Thierry's box of matches and struck a light. It flared, and he lit the candle with ease. In fact, everything about the room was perfectly normal; all the horrible conditions prevailing but a couple of hours ago had disappeared.

But where was Thierry? Carrying the lighted candle, he passed out of the door, and searched in the adjoining rooms. In one of them, to his relief, he found the Frenchman sleeping profoundly in an armchair.

Low touched his arm. Thierry leapt to his feet, fending off an imaginary blow with his arm. Then he turned his scared face on Low.

'What! You, Monsieur Flaxman! How have you escaped?'

'I should rather ask you how you escaped,' said Low, smiling at the havoc the night's experiences had worked on his friend's looks and spirits.

'I was crowded out of the room against the door. That infernal thing—what was it?—With its damp, swelling flesh, enclosed me!' A shudder of disgust stopped him. 'I was a fly in an aspic. I could not move. I sank into the stifling pulp. The air grew thick. I called to you, but your answers became inaudible. Then I was suddenly thrust against the door by a huge hand—it felt like one, at least. I had a struggle for my life, I was all but crushed, and then, I do not know how, I found myself outside the door. I shouted to you in vain. Therefore, as I could not help you, I came here, and—I will confess it, my dear friend—I locked and bolted the door. After some time I went again into the hall and listened; but, as I heard nothing, I resolved to wait until daylight and the return of Sir George.'

'That's all right,' said Low. 'It was an experience worth having.'

'But, no! Not for me! I do not envy you your researches into mysteries of this abominable description. I now comprehend perfectly that Sir George has lost his nerve if he has had to do with this horror. Besides, it is entirely impossible to explain these things.'

At this moment they heard Sir George's arrival, and went out to meet him.

'I could not sleep all night for thinking of you!' exclaimed Blackburton on seeing them; 'and I came along as soon as it was light. Something has happened.'

'But certainly something has happened,' cried M. Thierry shaking his head solemnly; 'something of the most bizarre, of the most horrible! Monsieur Flaxman, you shall tell Sir George this story. You have been in that accursed room all night, and remain alive to tell the tale!'

As Low came to the conclusion of the story, Sir George suddenly exclaimed:

'You have met with some injury to your face, Mr Low.'

Low turned to the mirror. In the now strong light three parallel weals from eyes to mouth could be seen.

'I remember a stinging pain like a lash on my cheek. What would you say these marks were caused by, Thierry?' asked Low.

Thierry looked at them and shook his head.

'No one in their senses would venture to offer any explanation of the occurrences of last night,' he replied.

'Something of this sort, do you think?' asked Low again, putting down the object he held in his hand on the table.

Thierry took it up and described it aloud.

'A long and thin object of a brown and yellow colour and twisted like a sabre-bladed corkscrew,' then he started slightly and glanced at Low.

'It's a human nail, I imagine,' suggested Low.

'But no human being has talons of this kind—except, perhaps, a Chinaman of high rank.'

'There are no Chinamen about here, nor ever have been, to my knowledge,' said Blackburton shortly. 'I'm very much afraid that, in spite of all you have so bravely faced, we are no nearer to any rational explanation.'

'On the contrary, I fancy I begin to see my way. I believe, after all, that I may be able to convert you, Thierry,' said Flaxman Low.

'Convert me?'

'To a belief in the definite aim of my work. But you shall judge for yourself. What do you make of it so far? I claim that you know as much of the matter as I do.'

'My dear good friend, I make nothing of it,' returned Thierry, shrugging his shoulders and spreading out his hands. 'Here we have a tissue of unprecedented incidents that can be explained on no theory whatever.'

'But this is definite,' and Flaxman Low held up the blackened nail.

'And how do you propose to connect that nail with the black hairs—with the eyes that looked through the bars of a cage—the fate of Batty, with its symptoms of death by pressure and suffocation—our experience of swelling flesh, that something which filled and filled the room to the exclusion of all else? How are you going to account for these things by any kind of connected hypothesis?' asked Thierry, with a shade of irony.

'I mean to try,' replied Low.

At lunch time Thierry inquired how the theory was getting on.

'It progresses,' answered Low. 'By the way, Sir George, who lived in this house for some time prior to, say, 1840? He was a man—it may have been a woman, but, from the nature of his studies, I am inclined to think it was a man—who was deeply read in ancient necromancy, Eastern magic, mesmerism, and subjects of a kindred nature. And was he not buried in the vault you pointed out?'

'Do you know anything more about him?' asked Sir George in surprise.

'He was, I imagine,' went on Flaxman Low reflectively, 'hirsute and swarthy, probably a recluse, and suffered from a morbid and extravagant fear of death.'

'How do you know all this?'

'I only asked about it. Am I right?'

'You have described my cousin, Sir Gilbert Blackburton, in every particular. I can show you his portrait in another room.'

As they stood looking at the painting of Sir Gilbert Blackburton, with his long, melancholy, olive face and thick, black beard, Sir George went on. 'My grandfather succeeded him at Yand. I have often heard my father speak of Sir Gilbert, and his strange studies and extraordinary fear of death. Oddly enough, in the end he died rather suddenly, while he was still hale and strong. He predicted his own approaching death, and had a doctor in attendance for a week or two before he died. He was placed in a coffin he had got made on some plan of his own, and buried in the vault. His death occurred in 1842 or 1843. If you care to see them I can show you some of his papers, which may interest you.'

Mr Flaxman Low spent the afternoon over the papers. When evening came, he rose from his work with a sigh of content, stretched himself, and joined Thierry and Sir George in the garden.

They dined at Lady Blackburton's, and it was late before Sir George found himself alone with Mr Flaxman Low and his friend.

'Have you formed any opinion about the thing which haunts the Manor House?' he asked anxiously.

Thierry elaborated a cigarette, crossed his legs, and added:

'If you have in truth come to any definite conclusion, pray let us hear it, my dear Monsieur Flaxman.'

'I have reached a very definite and satisfactory conclusion,' replied Low. 'The Manor House is haunted by Sir Gilbert Blackburton, who died, or, rather, who seemed to die, on the 15th of August, 1842.'

'Nonsense! The nail fifteen inches long at the least—how do you connect it with Sir Gilbert?' asked Blackburton testily.

'I am convinced that it belonged to Sir Gilbert,' Low answered.

'But the long black hair like a woman's?'

'Dissolution in the case of Sir Gilbert was not complete—not consummated, so to speak—as I hope to show you later. Even in the case of dead persons the hair and nails have been known to grow. By a rough calculation as to the growth of nails in such cases, I was enabled to indicate approximately the date of Sir Gilbert's death. The hair too grew on his head.'

'But the barred eyes? I saw them myself!' exclaimed the young man.

'The eyelashes grow also. You follow me?'

'You have, I presume, some theory in connection with this?' observed Thierry. 'It must be a very curious one.'

'Sir Gilbert in his fear of death appears to have mastered and elaborated a strange and ancient formula by which the grosser factors of the body being eliminated, the more ethereal portions continue to retain the spirit, and the body is thus preserved from absolute disintegration. In this manner true death may be indefinitely deferred. Secure from the ordinary chances and changes of existence, this spiritualized body could retain a modified life practically forever.'

'This is a most extraordinary idea, my dear fellow,' remarked Thierry.

'But why should Sir Gilbert haunt the Manor House, and one special room?'

'The tendency of spirits to return to the old haunts of bodily life is almost universal. We cannot yet explain the reason of this attraction of environment.'

'But the expansion the crowding substance which we ourselves felt? You cannot meet that difficulty,' said Thierry persistently.

'Not as fully as I could wish, perhaps. But the power of expanding and contracting to a degree far beyond our comprehension is a well-known attribute of spiritualized matter.'

'Wait one little moment, my dear Monsieur Flaxman,' broke in Thierry's voice after an interval; 'this is very clever and ingenious indeed. As a theory I give it my sincere admiration. But proof—proof is what we now demand.'

Flaxman Low looked steadily at the two incredulous faces.

'This,' he said slowly, 'is the hair of Sir Gilbert Blackburton, and this nail is from the little finger of his left hand. You can prove my assertion by opening the coffin.'

Sir George, who was pacing up and down the room impatiently, drew up.

'I don't like it at all, Mr Low, I tell you frankly. I don't like it at all. I see no object in violating the coffin. I am not concerned to verify this unpleasant theory of yours. I have only one desire; I want to get rid of this haunting presence, whatever it is.'

'If I am right,' replied Low, 'the opening of the coffin and exposure of the remains to strong sunshine for a short time will free you forever from this presence.'

In the early morning, when the summer sun struck warmly on the lawns of Yand, the three men carried the coffin from the vault to a quiet spot among the shrubs where, secure from observation, they raised the lid.

Within the coffin lay the semblance of Gilbert Blackburton, maned to the ears with long and coarse black hair. Matted eyelashes swept the fallen cheeks, and beside the body stretched the bony hands, each with its dependent sheaf of switch-like nails.

Low bent over and raised the left hand gingerly.

The little finger was without a nail!

Two hours later they came back and looked again. The sun had in the meantime done its work; nothing remained but a fleshless skeleton and a few half-rotten shreds of clothing.

The ghost of Yand Manor House has never since been heard of.

When Thierry bade Flaxman Low goodbye, he said:

'In time, my dear Monsieur Flaxman, you will add another to our sciences. You establish your facts too well for my peace of mind.'

THE VOICE IN THE NIGHT

W.H. Hodgson

It was a dark, starless night. We were becalmed in the Northern Pacific. Our exact position I do not know; for the sun had been hidden during the course of a weary, breathless week, by a thin haze which had seemed to float above us, about the height of our mastheads, at whiles descending and shrouding the surrounding sea.

With there being no wind, we had steadied the tiller, and I was the only man on deck. The crew, consisting of two men and a boy, were sleeping forward in their den; while Will—my friend, and the master of our little craft—was aft in his bunk on the port side of the little cabin.

Suddenly, from out of the surrounding darkness, there came a hail:

'Schooner, ahoy!'

The cry was so unexpected that I gave no immediate answer, because of my surprise.

It came again—a voice curiously throaty and inhuman, calling from somewhere upon the dark sea away on our port broadside:

'Schooner, ahoy!'

'Hullo!' I sung out, having gathered my wits somewhat. 'What are you? What do you want?'

'You need not be afraid,' answered the queer voice, having probably noticed some trace of confusion in my tone. 'I am only an old—man.'

The pause sounded oddly; but it was only afterwards that it came back to me with any significance.

'Why don't you come alongside, then?' I queried somewhat snappishly; for I liked not his hinting at my having been a trifle shaken.

'I—I—can't. It wouldn't be safe. I—' The voice broke off, and there was silence.

'What do you mean?' I asked, growing more and more astonished. 'Why not safe? Where are you?'

I listened for a moment; but there came no answer. And then, a sudden indefinite suspicion, of I knew not what, coming to me, I stepped swiftly to the binnacle, and took out the lighted lamp. At the same time, I knocked on the deck with my heel to waken Will. Then I was back at the side, throwing the yellow funnel of light out into the silent immensity beyond our rail. As I did so, I heard a slight, muffled cry, and then the sound of a splash as though someone had dipped oars abruptly. Yet I cannot say that I saw anything with certainty; save, it seemed to me, that with the first flash of the light, there had been something upon the waters, where now there was nothing.

'Hullo, there!' I called. 'What foolery is this!'

But there came only the indistinct sounds of a boat being pulled away into the night.

Then I heard Will's voice, from the direction of the after scuttle:

'What's up, George?'

'Come here, Will!' I said.

'What is it?' he asked, coming across the deck.

I told him the queer thing which had happened. He put several questions; then after a moment's silence, he raised his hands to his lips, and hailed:

'Boat, ahoy!'

From a long distance away there came back to us a faint reply, and my companion repeated his call. Presently, after a short period of silence, there grew on our hearing the muffled sound of oars; at which Will hailed again.

This time there was a reply:

'Put away the light.'

'I'm damned if I will,' I muttered; but Will told me to do as the voice bade, and I shoved it down under the bulwarks.

'Come nearer,' he said, and the oar-strokes continued. Then, when apparently some half-dozen fathoms distant, they again ceased.

'Come alongside,' exclaimed Will. 'There's nothing to be frightened of aboard here!'

'Promise that you will not show the light?'

'What's to do with you,' I burst out, 'that you're so infernally afraid of the light?'

'Because—' began the voice, and stopped short.

'Because what?' I asked quickly.

Will put his hand on my shoulder.

'Shut up a minute, old man,' he said, in a low voice. 'Let me tackle him.'

He leant more over the rail.

'See here, Mister,' he said, 'this is a pretty queer business, you coming upon us like this, right out in the middle of the blessed Pacific. How are we to know what sort of a hanky-panky trick you're up to? You say there's only one of you. How are we to know, unless we get a squint at you—eh? What's your objection to the light, anyway?'

As he finished, I heard the noise of the oars again, and then the voice came; but now from a greater distance, and sounding extremely hopeless and pathetic.

'I am sorry—sorry! I would not have troubled you, only I am hungry, and—so is she.'

The voice died away, and the sound of the oars, dipping irregularly, was borne to us.

'Stop!' sung out Will. 'I don't want to drive you away. Come back! We'll keep the light hidden, if you don't like it.'

He turned to me:

'It's a damned queer rig, this; but I think there's nothing to be afraid of?'

There was a question in his tone, and I replied:

'No, I think the poor devil's been wrecked around here, and gone crazy.'

The sound of the oars drew nearer.

'Shove that lamp back in the binnacle,' said Will; then he leaned over the rail and listened. I replaced the lamp, and came back to his side. The dipping of the oars ceased some dozen yards distant.

'Won't you come alongside now?' asked Will in an even voice. 'I have had the lamp put back in the binnacle.'

'I—I cannot,' replied the voice. 'I dare not come nearer. I dare not even pay you for the—the provisions.'

'That's all right,' said Will, and hesitated. 'You're welcome to as much grub as you can take—' Again he hesitated.

'You are very good,' exclaimed the voice. 'May God, Who understands everything, reward you—' It broke off huskily.

'The—the lady?' said Will abruptly. 'Is she—'

'I have left her behind upon the island,' came the voice.

'What island?' I cut in.

'I know not its name,' returned the voice. 'I would to God—!' it began, and checked itself as suddenly.

'Could we not send a boat for her?' asked Will at this point.

'No!' said the voice, with extraordinary emphasis. 'My God! No!' There was a moment's pause; then it added, in a tone which seemed a merited reproach:

'It was because of our want I ventured—because her agony tortured me.'

'I am a forgetful brute,' exclaimed Will. 'Just wait a minute, whoever you are, and I will bring you up something at once.'

In a couple of minutes he was back again, and his arms were full of various edibles. He paused at the rail.

'Can't you come alongside for them?' he asked.

'No—I *dare not,*' replied the voice, and it seemed to me that in its tones I detected a note of stifled craving—as though the owner hushed a mortal desire. It came to me then in a flash, that the poor old creature out there in the darkness, was *suffering* for actual need of that which Will held in his arms; and yet, because of some unintelligible dread, refraining from dashing to the side of our little schooner, and receiving it. And with the lightning-like conviction, there came the knowledge that the Invisible was not mad; but sanely facing some intolerable horror.

'Damn it, Will!' I said, full of many feelings, over which predominated a vast sympathy. 'Get a box. We must float off the stuff to him in it.'

This we did—propelling it away from the vessel, out into the darkness, by means of a boathook. In a minute, a slight cry from the Invisible came to us, and we knew that he had secured the box.

A little later, he called out a farewell to us, and so heartful a blessing, that I am sure we were the better for it. Then, without more ado, we heard the ply of oars across the darkness.

'Pretty soon off,' remarked Will, with perhaps just a little sense of injury.

'Wait,' I replied. 'I think somehow he'll come back. He must have been badly needing that food.'

'And the lady,' said Will. For a moment he was silent; then he continued:

'It's the queerest thing ever I've tumbled across, since I've been fishing.'

'Yes,' I said, and fell to pondering.

And so the time slipped away—an hour, another, and still Will stayed with me; for the queer adventure had knocked all desire for sleep out of him.

The third hour was three parts through, when we heard again the sound of oars across the silent ocean.

'Listen!' said Will, a low note of excitement in his voice.

'He's coming, just as I thought,' I muttered.

The dipping of the oars grew nearer, and I noted that the strokes were firmer and longer. The food had been needed.

They came to a stop a little distance off the broadside, and the queer voice came again to us through the darkness:

'Schooner, ahoy!'

'That you?' asked Will.

'Yes,' replied the voice. 'I left you suddenly; but—but there was great need.'

'The lady?' questioned Will.

'The—lady is grateful now on earth. She will be more grateful soon in—in heaven.'

Will began to make some reply, in a puzzled voice; but became confused, and broke off short. I said nothing. I was wondering at the curious pauses, and, apart from my wonder, I was full of a great sympathy.

The voice continued:

'We—she and I, have talked, as we shared the result of God's tenderness and yours—'

Will interposed; but without coherence.

'I beg of you not to—to belittle your deed of Christian charity this night,' said the voice. 'Be sure that it has not escaped His notice.'

It stopped, and there was a full minute's silence. Then it came again:

'We have spoken together upon that which—which has befallen us. We had thought to go out, without telling any, of the terror which has come into our lives. She is with me in believing that tonight's happenings are under a special ruling, and that it is God's wish that we should tell to you all that we have suffered since—since—'

'Yes?' said Will softly.

'Since the sinking of the *Albatross*.'

'Ah!' I exclaimed involuntarily. 'She left Newcastle for 'Frisco some six months ago, and hasn't been heard of since.'

'Yes,' answered the voice. 'But some few degrees to the North of the line she was caught in a terrible storm, and dismasted. When the day came, it was found that she was leaking badly, and, presently, it falling to a calm, the sailors took to the boats, leaving—leaving a young lady—my fiancèe—and myself upon the wreck.

'We were below, gathering together a few of our belongings, when they left. They were entirely callous, through fear, and when we came up upon the decks, we saw them only as small shapes afar off upon the horizon. Yet we did not despair, but set to work and constructed a small raft. Upon this we put such few matters as it would hold, including a quantity of water and some ship's biscuit. Then, the vessel being very deep in the water, we got ourselves on to the raft, and pushed off.

'It was later, when I observed that we seemed to be in the way of some tide or current which bore us from the ship at an angle; so that in the course of three hours, by my watch, her hull became invisible to our sight, her broken masts remaining in view for a somewhat longer period. Then, toward evening, it grew misty, and so through the night. The next day we were still encompassed by the mist, the weather remaining quiet.

'For four days we drifted through this strange haze, until, on the evening of the fourth day, there grew upon our ears the murmur of breakers at a distance. Gradually it became plainer, and, somewhat after midnight, it appeared to sound upon either hand at no very great space. The raft was raised upon a swell several times, and then we were in smooth water, and the noise of the breakers was behind.

'When the morning came, we found that we were in a sort of great lagoon; but of this we noticed little at the time; for close before us, through the enshrouding mist, loomed the hull of a large sailing-vessel. With one accord, we fell upon our knees and thanked God; for we thought that here was an end to our perils. We had much to learn.

'The raft drew near to the ship, and we shouted on them to take us aboard; but none answered. Presently the raft touched against the side of the vessel, and, seeing a rope hanging downwards, I seized it and began to climb. Yet I had much ado to make my way up, because of a kind of grey, lichenous fungus which had seized upon the rope, and which blotched the side of the ship lividly.

'I reached the rail and clambered over it, on to the deck. Here I saw that the decks were covered, in great patches, with the grey masses, some of them rising into nodules several feet in height; but at the time I thought less of this matter than of the possibility of there being people aboard the ship. I shouted; but none answered. Then I went to the door below the poop deck. I opened it, and peered in. There was a great smell of staleness, so that I knew in a moment that nothing living was within, and with the knowledge, I shut the door quickly; for I felt suddenly lonely.

'I went back to the side where I had scrambled up. My—my sweetheart was still sitting quietly upon the raft. Seeing me look down, she called up to know whether there were any aboard of the ship. I replied that the vessel had the appearance of having been long deserted; but that if she would wait a little I would see whether there was anything in the shape of a ladder by which she could ascend to the deck. Then we would make a search through the vessel together. A little later on the opposite side of the decks, I found a rope side-ladder. This I carried across, and a minute afterwards she was beside me.

'Together we explored the cabins and apartments in the after part of the ship; but nowhere was there any sign of life. Here and there, within the cabins themselves, we came across odd patches of that queer fungus; but this, as my sweetheart said, could be cleansed away.

'In the end, having assured ourselves that the after portion of the vessel was empty, we picked our ways to the bows, between the ugly grey nodules of that strange growth; and here we made a further search, which told us that there was indeed none aboard but ourselves.

'This being now beyond any doubt, we returned to the stern of the ship and proceeded to make ourselves as comfortable as possible. Together we cleared out and cleaned two of the cabins; and after that I made examination whether there was anything eatable in the ship. This I soon found was so, and thanked God in my heart for His goodness. In addition to this I discovered the whereabouts of the freshwater pump, and having fixed it I found the water drinkable, though somewhat unpleasant to the taste.

'For several days we stayed aboard the ship, without attempting to get to the shore. We were busily engaged in making the place habitable. Yet even thus early we became aware that our lot was even less to be desired than might have been imagined; for though, as a first step, we scraped away the odd patches of growth that studded the floors and walls of the cabins and saloon, yet they returned almost to their original size within the space of twenty-four hours, which not only discouraged us, but gave us a feeling of vague unease.

'Still we would not admit ourselves beaten, so set to work afresh, and not only scraped away the fungus, but soaked the places where it had been, with carbolic, a can-full of which I had found in the pantry. Yet, by the end of the week the growth had returned in full strength, and, in addition, it had spread to other places, as though our touching it had allowed germs from it to travel elsewhere.

'On the seventh morning, my sweetheart woke to find a small patch of it growing on her pillow, close to her face. At that, she came to me, so soon as she could get her garments upon her. I was in the galley at the time lighting the fire for breakfast.

'"Come here, John," she said, and led me aft. When I saw the thing upon her pillow I shuddered, and then and there we agreed to go right out of the ship and see whether we could not fare to make ourselves more comfortable ashore.

'Hurriedly we gathered together our few belongings, and even among these I found that the fungus had been at work; for one of her shawls had a little lump of it growing near one edge. I threw the whole thing over the side, without saying anything to her.

'The raft was still alongside, but it was too clumsy to guide, and I lowered down a small boat that hung across the stern, and in this we made our way to the shore. Yet, as we drew near to it, I became gradually aware that here the vile fungus, which had driven us from the ship, was growing riot. In places it rose into horrible, fantastic mounds, which seemed almost to quiver, as with a quiet life, when the wind blew across them. Here and there it took on the forms of vast fingers, and in others it just spread out flat and smooth and treacherous. Odd places, it appeared as grotesque stunted trees, seeming extraordinarily kinked and gnarled—the whole quaking vilely at times.

'At first, it seemed to us that there was no single portion of the surrounding shore which was not hidden beneath the masses of the hideous lichen; yet, in this, I found we were mistaken; for somewhat later, coasting along the shore at a little distance, we descried a smooth white patch of what appeared to be fine sand, and there we landed. It was not sand. What it was I do not know. All that I have observed is that upon it the fungus will not grow; while everywhere else, save where the sand-like earth wanders oddly, path-wise, amid the grey desolation of the lichen, there is nothing but that loathsome greyness.

'It is difficult to make you understand how cheered we were to find one place that was absolutely free from the growth, and here we deposited our belongings. Then we went back to the ship for such things as it seemed to us we should need. Among other matters, I managed to bring ashore with me one of the ship's sails, with which I constructed two small tents, which, though exceedingly rough-shaped, served the purposes for which they were intended. In these we lived and stored our various necessities, and thus for a matter of some four weeks all went smoothly and without particular unhappiness. Indeed, I may say with much of happiness—for—for we were together.

'It was on the thumb of her right hand that the growth first showed. It was only a small circular spot, much like a little grey mole. My God! How the fear leapt to my heart when she showed me the place. We cleansed it, between us, washing it with carbolic and water. In the morning of the following day she showed her hand to me again. The grey warty thing had returned. For a little while, we looked at one another in silence. Then, still wordless, we started again to remove it. In the midst of the operation she spoke suddenly.

'"What's that on the side of your face, dear?" Her voice was sharp with anxiety. I put my hand up to feel.

'"There! Under the hair by your ear. A little to the front a bit." My finger rested upon the place, and then I knew.

'"Let us get your thumb done first," I said. And she submitted, only because she was afraid to touch me until it was cleansed. I finished washing and disinfecting her thumb, and then she turned to my face. After it was finished we sat together and talked awhile of many things; for there had come into our lives sudden, very terrible thoughts. We were, all at once, afraid of something worse than death. We spoke of loading the boat with provisions and water and making our way out on to the sea; yet we were helpless, for many causes, and—and the growth had attacked us already. We decided to stay. God would do with us what was His will. We would wait.

'A month, two months, three months passed and the places grew somewhat, and there had come others. Yet we fought so strenuously with the fear that its headway was but slow, comparatively speaking.

'Occasionally we ventured off to the ship for such stores as we needed. There we found that the fungus grew persistently. One of the nodules on the main deck became soon as high as my head.

'We had now given up all thought or hope of leaving the island. We had realized that it would be unallowable to go among healthy humans, with the things from which we were suffering.

'With this determination and knowledge in our minds we knew that we should have to husband our food and water; for we did not know, at that time, but that we should possibly live for many years.

'This reminds me that I have told you that I am an old man. Judged by years this is not so. But-but-'

He broke off; then continued somewhat abruptly:

'As I was saying, we knew that we should have to use care in the matter of food. But we had no idea then how little food there was left, of which to take care. It was a week later that I made the discovery that all the other bread tanks—which I had supposed full—were empty, and that (beyond odd tins of vegetables and meat, and some other matters) we had nothing on which to depend, but the bread in the tank which I had already opened.

'After learning this I bestirred myself to do what I could, and set to work at fishing in the lagoon; but with no success. At this I was somewhat inclined to feel desperate until the thought came to me to try outside the lagoon, in the open sea.

'Here, at times, I caught odd fish; but so infrequently that they proved of but little help in keeping us from the hunger which threatened. It seemed to me that our deaths were likely to come by hunger, and not by the growth of the thing which had seized upon our bodies.

'We were in this state of mind when the fourth month wore out. 'Then I made a very horrible discovery. One morning, a little before midday, I came off from the ship with a portion of the biscuits which were left. In the mouth of her tent I saw my sweetheart sitting, eating something.

'"What is it, my dear?" I called out as I leapt ashore. Yet, on hearing my voice, she seemed confused, and, turning, slyly threw something towards the edge of the little clearing. It fell short, and a vague suspicion having arisen within me, I walked across and picked it up. It was a piece of the grey fungus.

'As I went to her with it in my hand, she turned deadly pale; then a rose red.

'I felt strangely dazed and frightened.

'"My dear! My dear!" I said, and could say no more. Yet at my words she broke down and cried bitterly. Gradually, as she calmed, I got from her the news that she had tried it the preceding day, and—and liked it. I got her to promise on her knees not to touch it again, however great our hunger. After she had promised she told me that the desire for it had come suddenly, and that, until the moment of desire, she had experienced nothing towards it but the most extreme repulsion.

'Later in the day, feeling strangely restless, and much shaken with the thing which I had discovered, I made my way along one of the twisted paths—formed by the white, sand-like substance—which led among the fungoid growth. I had, once before, ventured along there; but not to any great distance. This time, being involved in perplexing thought, I went much farther than hitherto.

'Suddenly I was called to myself by a queer, hoarse sound on my left. Turning quickly I saw that there was movement among an extraordinarily shaped mass of fungus, close to my elbow. It was swaying uneasily, as though it possessed life of its own. Abruptly, as I stared, the thought came to me that the thing had a grotesque resemblance to the figure of a distorted human creature. Even as the fancy flashed into my brain, there was a slight, sickening noise of tearing, and I saw that one of the branch-like arms was detaching itself from the surrounding grey masses, and coming towards me. The head of the thing—a shapeless grey ball, inclined in my direction. I stood stupidly, and the vile arm brushed across my face. I gave out a frightened cry, and ran back a few paces. There was a sweetish taste upon my lips where the thing had touched me. I licked them, and was immediately filled with an inhuman desire. I turned and seized a mass of the fungus. Then more, and—more. I was insatiable. In the midst of devouring, the remembrance of the morning's discovery swept into my mazed brain. It was sent by God. I dashed the fragment I held to the ground. Then, utterly wretched and feeling a dreadful guiltiness, I made my way back to the little encampment.

'I think she knew, by some marvellous intuition which love must have given, so soon as she set eyes on me. Her quiet sympathy made it easier for me, and I told her of my sudden weakness; yet omitted to mention the extraordinary thing which had gone before. I desired to spare her all unnecessary terror.

'But, for myself, I had added an intolerable knowledge, to breed an incessant terror in my brain; for I doubted not but that I had seen the end of one of those men who had come to the island in the ship in the lagoon; and in that monstrous ending I had seen our own.

'Thereafter we kept from the abominable food, though the desire for it had entered into our blood. Yet our drear punishment was upon us; for, day by day, with monstrous rapidity, the fungoid growth took hold of our poor bodies. Nothing we could do would check it materially, and so—and so—we who had been human, became—well, it matters less each day. Only—only we had been man and maid!

And day by day, the fight is more dreadful, to withstand the hunger-lust for the terrible lichen.

'A week ago we ate the last of the biscuit, and since that time

I have caught three fish. I was out here fishing tonight, when your schooner drifted upon me out of the mist. I hailed you. You know the rest, and may God, out of His great heart, bless you for your goodness to a—a couple of poor outcast souls.'

There was the dip of an oar—another. Then the voice came again, and for the last time, sounding through the slight surrounding mist, ghostly and mournful.

'God bless you! Goodbye.'

'Goodbye,' we shouted together, hoarsely, our hearts full of many emotions. I glanced about me. I became aware that the dawn was upon us.

The sun flung a stray beam across the hidden sea; pierced the mist dully, and lit up the receding boat with a gloomy fire. Indistinctly, I saw something nodding between the oars. I thought of a sponge—a great, grey nodding sponge. The oars continued to ply. They were grey—as was the boat—and my eyes searched a moment vainly for the conjunction of hand and oar. My gaze flashed back to the—head. It nodded forward as the oars went backward for the stroke. Then the oars were dipped, the boat shot out of the patch of light, and the—the thing went nodding into the mist.

THE ARYAN SMILES

J. Warton and N. Blenman

It shall ever be one of my greatest regrets that I did not go with Michael Clancey on the evening he met his untimely death. If I had not been able to prevent it, I might, at least, have consoled a pious widow and daughter with the thought that his soul still lingered for the charity of their prayers, and that his end had not been the awful one of suicide. Not that they inclined to the latter view, but they feared it, while, with the mentality of simple Irish Catholics, they naturally acquiesced in the superstitious explanation of a very bizarre incident.

Whereas I might, then, have been able to bring into the light of human reason at least one of these happenings in a community where too ready a credence is placed in the damnable black arts of the Orient, it is to a mind, sceptical and materialistic as mine, the more galling to have to relate only the remarkable facts concerning the loss of a very dear friend.

'Mike,' I had said, 'I can't go with you tonight, much as I would love to have a drive'—and much as I liked his company; for we used to spend many an evening chatting about our military days, and Mike, bluff and quick-tempered, had been the most popular man in the Battery.

We had come to India together, and like so many soldiers in the old days, we had been glad to take up quieter occupations and to remain in the country. The growing railway systems offered a good field for employment, and my friend had joined the Southern Punjab and Delhi Railway; on this comparatively small section of railroad, he had had a somewhat meteoric career. As Station Master of Delhi, and a man not yet forty-five, he had reason to exult in his change of professions, for he might otherwise have been plain Farrier-Sergeant Clancey.

I had been lucky to get in with a firm of piece goods merchants.

One of our more important men was up from Calcutta, and as I had a semi-business dinner to attend that evening, I did not feel quite up to the conviviality which Michael Clancey would be sure to lead me into: although there was time for a little outing before dinner, I had preferred to entertain him at my bungalow. After a half-hour's tête-à-tête and a couple of mild whiskies on the verandah, he had climbed into his dog-cart alone, cracked his whip and turned sharply out my gate. It was a sultry July evening. Before going in to dress, I stood outside for a few minutes listening to the fine even patter of his Waler's hoofs get fainter and fainter down the long quiet road. I had seen and heard the last of Mike Clancey for ever, but did not know it then.

It must have been 7.30 when he left me; an hour later I was at the hotel at which I was to dine. Four of us sat down to dinner.

We were well into our cigars when I received the following note. On top of the small envelope was written 'Urgent, Please deliver at once.' Excusing myself, I read—

Dear Mr Warton,—Mr Clancey's syce, who is the bearer

of this, will tell you more than I can. Being a friend of Mr Clancey's, I am sure you will question the man at once. I am nervous about it myself, and shall tell you the reasons for my anxiety if you would call over now.

Yours sincerely, Marie Smythe

Mrs Smythe was one of the Railway colony. I think her husband was the platelayer. My friend was boarding with the Smythes at the time while his wife and daughter were in the hills.

Somewhat disconcerted at receiving this vague note, I crumpled it into my pocket, and, leaving the company as nicely as I could, went downstairs to hear what the groom had to say. He had come down in his master's dog-cart; the horse was champing and sneezing over his head while he gave me a story, which, coupled with Mrs Smythe's note, was sufficiently alarming, although the whole affair bore a very queer aspect indeed.

For a time I wondered whether it warranted my leaving the dinner party. I told the syce to wait, however, and went back to my fellow-diners for a few minutes and even had another drink. Being uneasy all the time, and as it was nearly ten o'clock, I decided at last to go. Saying boldly that a friend had been suddenly taken ill, and receiving from each one a laconic 'I'm sorry!' as he rose to shake hands, I bid my companions 'Goodnight.'

Sitting by the syce, while he drove me to Mrs Smythe's, I got him to recount his brief story.

'The Sahib went out first at seven o'clock,' he said.

'Yes, yes,' I put in, 'he came to see me.'

'Well, he returned home, called for the whisky, sat a while on the chabutra, and then we drove off towards the Roshanara Gardens. Sahib often went there before dinner "to take the air". He would walk round the Gardens, leaving me to hold the horse. This evening, I thought it rather late for the Master's usual drive. However, it was still lightsome when he pulled up in the Gardens. He alighted and went off in the direction of the tank. Holding the reins, I sat down on the gravel walk. But the Sahib being longer than I thought he would, I eventually took the horse and buggy a few paces off on to the lawn, where I secured the reins to a small tree, gave the animal his fodder from the cart, and began to smoke myself.

'In this way, Sahib, I had consumed two or three "bins", strolling about some times to see if the master was in sight; and the horse meanwhile had finished his bag of hay.

'There was no sign of the Sahib, and we must have been out more than an hour—he usually dined by half-past-eight—so I walked all round the Gardens. After waiting another short while, I drove back to the kothi without him, then inquired at Smythe Memsahib's, who sent me back to the Gardens at once to look for my Master; but I did not stay there more than a few minutes. To tell you the truth, Sahib, we poor country folk are very frightened. And what was the use of waiting? So I went again to the Memsahib, after having called first at your house; and then she gave me the letter to you.'

To such a narrative I had no comments to make, and waited rather curiously for Mrs Smythe's account, which she gave me in the presence of her husband.

'We stayed dinner very long for Mr Clancey,' she said, after apologizing for having called me away. This, she said, she would not have done but for the fact that Mr Clancey had been rather unwell during the day.

'Oh,' I remarked, 'I didn't know that. He seemed all right when I saw him this evening.'

'It's a funny thing, Mr Warton,' she went on. 'A kind of fit, perhaps; though I have never seen anything like it before. At breakfast Mr Clancey complained of feeling very hot. He said his skin was burning. I suggested "prickly heat"; but he assured me it wasn't that, and began to eat quite heartily. Suddenly we saw his face go as red as a turkey-cock's; he jumped from the table, tearing off his collar and unbuttoning his coat. "Fiends alive, Fiends alive, Mrs Smythe!" he shouted, grabbing at his clothes. "I'll go home!"

"No, go into the bedroom, Mr Clancey," I said. "What's the matter?"

Throwing off his coat, he went inside, supported by my husband.'

'With his shirt off,' added Mr Smythe, 'he ran straight to the bathroom, and ducked his head in the tub. "I'm on fire, Smythe," he cried. "Splash it on hard!" and we drenched him to the waist with mugfuls of cold water, you could see the very blood glowing under his skin, but it soon got back its natural whiteness, and he sat down with us and finished his meal.'

Mrs Smythe continued the account.

'We saw him again at tea time,' she told me. 'He had just come from his round at the station, as usual. He ate very little, but drank an enormous quantity of tea, saying there was nothing like tea for cooling the system. It has been a very hot day, as you know, and we did not think too much of Mr Clancey's discomfort. However, I took his temperature before he went home; he had no fever.'

'In that case,' I said, rising impatiently, 'it might be that poor Clancey is lying in an apoplectic fit, or something of the kind—I wonder whether this man looked properly!—I had better go to the Gardens and see.'

Smythe offered to accompany me, and we set off to the Roshanara Gardens. On the way I had more details of my friend's misfortune.

'My wife had not time to tell you,' began Smythe, 'but what has been troubling her most is damn queer—the sort of thing you might have no patience with; I have little time myself for these tales—but I may as well tell it to you. Now, these queer symptoms of Clancey's, when he complained of his flesh being on fire—these maybe anything at all. But he told us blandly that he thought it was the jogi's curse.'

'The jogi's curse?' I said.

'Yes,' reiterated Smythe, 'the jogi's curse. And when he said this, my wife became very solemn, telling him it was not right to jest about such things. But let me explain.

'Now, you know how hot-headed Clancey is. It appears that last evening he maltreated one of these religious mendicants—he told us about it at dinner. He was driving through the station garden when he noticed this sadhu fellow on the grass-plot. The man had set up a few bricks, lit a fire, and was preparing his evening meal. What Clancey said to him I don't know, and he probably had good reason to be annoyed, for he has practically made that garden with his own hands; but he should not have struck the fellow—though he told us about it very sadly afterwards. As a matter of fact, he is too fond of that horsewhip of his, using it on the station staff at times; in spite of it, they are fond of him. Anyhow, he says the jogi was insolent, that he laughed and went on with his cooking. The Station Master riled that his authority should be so flouted, dismounted from his dog-cart, whip in hand, and ordered the trespasser out of the garden; when he still would not go, Clancey lashed the smiling Hindu three or four times across the back. The jogi poured some water on to the fire, and, drawing out the moistened ashes from his chulah, threw it in handfuls over his naked body, applying the emolient especially to his smarting wounds. Then, holding up his skinny hands and pointing heavenward, he muttered something which the Irishman took to be oaths and curses. He says the man finally gathered up his things, spat on the ground, and went away, but not without looking round at Clancey and saying: "The Almighty has a Lash of Retribution! Its thongs are Flames of Fire!"'

'But,' I protested, 'Clancey wouldn't understand all that.'

'I believe one of his babus overheard, and translated it for him,' explained Smythe.

'An eloquent piece of nonsense!' I said. 'But, of course, it's just possible Clancey has been ailing from the weather. It has been a particularly hot day.'

In this part of India the monsoon is often very feeble. Here we were at the end of July, and still panting for the rain. The sky, however, had been overcast all day, which made the heat more unbearable.

It was pitchy dark in the Gardens; but with the aid of a couple of railway lanterns, we eventually went over the grounds very thoroughly by eleven o'clock. During this search Smythe and I walked right under a huge peepul tree that grew on the verge of the tank. Under this tree we missed the light from the second lantern, and, calling to the syce who carried it behind us, we saw that he stood some distance away. He said that he would not go under that tree for love or money, and begged that we would not ask him to do so. So Smythe took the lamp from him, and we passed on after examining the ground under the tree, as we did with every other dark patch and corner of the Gardens.

There was nothing for it now but to begin a long vigil on the spot where my friend had left his dog-cart, when he had commenced his walk. About midnight Smythe went home to his wife, so I was left with the syce for company. He sat cross-legged on the grass near me, while I reclined on the cushion seat which had been removed from the trap.

Feeling the urge to engage him in conversation, there was one question that came to me at once. (The more important matter of his master's encounter with the jogi we had already thrashed out; he had been with Clancey at the time and corroborated that story). In fact, the question I put to my companion now was just an idle one, for I guessed the likely answer, knowing the minds of these rustic folk regarding such things as phantoms and spooks. The tree he had been so afraid of, I thought, is probably haunted by a she-devil, the well-known churail. Anyhow, 'Syce,' I said, 'why wouldn't you come under that peepul tree with us?'

'No Hindu would, Sahib,' he answered, 'unless he were a stranger in Delhi.'

'No? And why not?'

'How shall I tell you? You white people laugh at these things. But you must have heard it when you were under the tree.'

'Heard what?'

'Didn't you hear him smoking his hookah?... T-oor-r-... T-oo-r-r-r?'

'What?' I said. 'In the branches of the tree? That was a night-bird of some kind!' And I laughed.

'For this reason,' he said indignantly, 'I did not wish to say anything about the cursed tree.'

However certain I felt that this simple-minded Hindu had mistaken the croaking of some nocturnal creature for the bubbling and gurgling drawl of a hookah, I was ready to hear any old story, and cajoled him into telling me a rather good one.

'In the first place,' I said, 'why do you call it a cursed tree? The peepul is sacred to you Hindus.'

'Yes,' he agreed, 'but this particular peepul has been cursed. It came about in this way: in the time of Emperor Aurungzeb, a certain pir took up this abode under this tree, and began to persecute the poor Hindu people who used to come to the sacred tree to offer their poojahs and to bathe in the tank. He would throw away the flowers, sweets and fruits of their sacrifices, desecrate their altars, and beat the devotees off if necessary.'

'The Hindus,' I commented, 'were very meek to allow the high-handed behaviour of this Mohamedan!'

'You know the fanatical Muslim Aurungzeb was,' he said. 'The poor Hindus could hope for no redress. And so things went on at this peepul tree, till, making a virtue of necessity, the Hindus of the neighbourhood abandoned their sacred tree to this wicked man. In fact, their veneration grew to loathing—it was considered to have been defiled. And when, eventually, the holy pir was buried on the spot where he had made his home, under the tree for some forty years, the curse was thought to be complete, and no Hindu would think of sacrificing under this peepul. One night, they say, a band of daring youths (Hindus) went to the pir's grave, exhumed the recently-interred body, and threw it into the tank, where it remained. Since then, Sahib, the soul of that wretched pir haunts the old peepul. I heard him tonight, worse luck! You heard him too. And he is always there at the top of the tree at night, pulling away at his hubble-bubble.'

'Humph!' I said, and thought I would like to go over to the tree and throw a few stones at the croaking bird which had given rise to the syce's funny story. I might have made the test, but that we had to take shelter presently under an open pavilion nearby, for the long-promised rain had come at last, though at an awkward time. A high wind blew the sand into our faces, there were quick flashes of lurid lightning, and we had only just enough time to unyoke the Waler before we realized that we were exposed to an Indian sandstorm. I thought the horse would have kicked down the wooden posts of the pavilion, and that the zinc roof would have been blown over our heads, while we struggled to make the animal share the small shelter with us. Soon the elements became calmer, and so did the horse. But suddenly, as if from nowhere, there was a bluish-yellow flash and a crashing report. Looking in the direction of the sound, I heard a splashing.

'Sahib,' whispered the syce, with his hand on my arm, 'that is the peepul tree! It has been struck!'

These sandstorms are fiercer than they are lasting, so in a few minutes we were able to go out and examine the tree, the syce keeping at a very safe distance. Almost half of it had been torn down and lay immersed in the water of the tank. The other part stood gaunt and lifeless on a charred and blackened trunk. This was easily discernible, for the bark of the peepul is of a glistening light grey colour.

I had had enough of strange stories, and now had come an uncanny experience. How this fitted into a chain of apparently occult influences was shown the next morning. After an anxious night of waiting and watching, informing the police, and having no rest, we began dredging operations at the tank; the clue for the search was Clancey's horsewhip.

Like a lost fishing-rod, it was seen to be sticking up out of the weeds close to the fallen tree. The syce recognized it at once; he said the Sahib always took the whip with him in these little walks.

About midway the body of my poor friend was brought out, with all the ordinary signs of drowning apparent. The water was certainly weedy; yet Clancey could swim well. But how and why he got into the water shall never be known. And just before his body was found, one of the men brought up a vessel covered over and filled with a loamy black soil from the bottom of the tank; when the mud was removed, the object revealed itself to be an old copper hookah.

'Throw it back!' cried the syce. 'It belonged to the wicked pir!'

Whether he was right or not will also never be known.

THE DOLL'S GHOST

F. Marion Crawford

It was a terrible accident, and for one moment the splendid machinery of Cranston House got out of gear and stood still. The butler emerged from the retirement in which he spent his elegant leisure, two grooms of the chambers appeared simultaneously from opposite directions, there were actually housemaids on the grand staircase, and those who remember the facts most exactly assert that Mrs Pringle herself positively stood upon the landing. Mrs Pringle was the housekeeper. As for the head nurse, the under nurse and the nursery-maid, their feelings cannot be described.

The Lady Gwendolen Lancaster-Douglas-Scroop, youngest daughter of the ninth Duke of Cranston, and aged six years and three months, picked herself up quite alone, and sat down on the third step of the grand staircase in Cranston House.

'Oh!' ejaculated the butler, and he disappeared again.

'Ah!' responded the grooms of the chambers, as they also went away.

'It's only that doll,' Mrs Pringle was distinctly heard to say, in a tone of contempt.

The under nurse heard her say it. Then the three nurses

gathered round Lady Gwendolen and patted her, and gave her unhealthy things out of their pockets, and hurried her out of Cranston House as fast as they could, lest it should be found out upstairs that they had allowed the Lady Gwendolen Lancaster-Douglas-Scroop to tumble down the grand staircase with her doll in her arms. And as the doll was badly broken, the nursery-maid carried it, with the pieces wrapped up in Lady Gwendolen's little cloak. It was not far to Hyde Park, and when they had reached a quiet place they took means to find out that Lady Gwendolen had no bruises. For the carpet was very thick and soft, and there was thick stuff under it to make it softer.

Lady Gwendolen Lancaster-Douglas-Scroop sometimes yelled, but she never cried. It was because she had yelled that the nurse had allowed her to go downstairs alone with Nina, the doll, under one arm, while she steadied herself with her other hand on the balustrade, and trod upon the polished marble steps beyond the edge of the carpet. So she had fallen, and Nina had come to grief.

◆

Mr Bernard Puckler and his little daughter lived in a little house in a little alley, which led out off a quiet little street not very far from Belgrave Square. He was the great doll doctor, and his extensive practice lay in the most aristocratic quarter. He mended dolls of all sizes and ages, boy dolls and girl dolls, baby dolls in long clothes, and grown-up dolls in fashionable gowns, talking dolls and dumb dolls, those that shut their eyes when they lay down, and those whose eyes had to be shut for them by means of a mysterious wire. His daughter Else was only just over twelve years old, but she was already very clever at mending dolls' clothes, and at doing their hair, which is harder than you might think, though the dolls sit quite still while it is being done.

Mr Puckler had originally been a German, but he had dissolved his nationality in the ocean of London many years ago, like a great many foreigners. He still had one or two German friends, however, who came on Saturday evenings and smoked with him and played picquet or 'skat' with him for farthing points, and called him 'Herr Doktor', which seemed to please Mr Puckler very much.

He looked older than he was, for his beard was rather long and ragged, his hair was grizzled and thin, and he wore horn-rimmed spectacles.

As for Else, she was a thin, pale child, very quiet and neat, with dark eyes and brown hair that was plaited down her back and tied with a bit of black ribbon. She mended the dolls' clothes and took the dolls back to their homes when they were quite strong again.

The house was a little one, but too big for the two people who lived in it. There was a small sitting-room on the street, and the workshop was at the back, and there were three rooms upstairs.

But the father and daughter lived most of their time in the workshop, because they were generally at work, even in the evenings.

Mr Puckler laid Nina on the table and looked at her a long time, till the tears began to fill his eyes behind the horn-rimmed spectacles. He was a very susceptible man, and he often fell in love with the dolls he mended, and found it hard to part with them when they had smiled at him for a few days. They were real little people to him, with characters and thoughts and feelings of their own, and he was very tender with them all. But some attracted him especially from the first, and when they were brought to him maimed and injured, their state seemed so pitiful to him that the tears came easily. You must remember that he had lived among dolls during a great part of his life, and understood them.

'How do you know that they feel nothing?' he went on to say to Else. 'You must be gentle with them. It costs nothing to be kind to the little beings, and perhaps it makes a difference to them.'

And Else understood him, because she was a child, and she knew that she was more to him than all the dolls.

He fell in love with Nina at first sight, perhaps because her beautiful brown glass eyes were something like Else's own, and he loved Else first and best, with all his heart. And, besides, it was a very sorrowful case. Nina had evidently not been long in the world, for her complexion was perfect, her hair was smooth where it should be smooth, and curly where it should be curly, and her silk clothes were perfectly new. But across her face was that frightful gash, like a sabre-cut, deep and shadowy within, but clean and sharp at the edges. When he tenderly pressed her head to close the gaping wound, the edges made a fine, grating sound, that was painful to hear, and the lids of the dark eyes quivered and trembled as though Nina were suffering dreadfully.

'Poor Nina!' he exclaimed sorrowfully. 'But I shall not hurt you much, though you will take a long time to get strong.'

He always asked the names of the broken dolls when they were brought to him, and sometimes the people knew what the children called them, and told him. He liked 'Nina' for a name. Altogether and in every way she pleased him more than any doll he had seen for many years, and he felt drawn to her, and made up his mind to make her perfectly strong and sound, no matter how much labour it might cost him.

Mr Puckler worked patiently a little at a time, and Else

watched him. She could do nothing for poor Nina, whose clothes needed no mending. The longer the doll doctor worked the more fond he became of the yellow hair and the beautiful brown glass eyes. He sometimes forgot all the other dolls that were waiting to be mended, lying side by side on a shelf, and sat for an hour gazing at Nina's face, while he racked his ingenuity for some new invention by which to hide even the smallest trace of the terrible accident.

She was wonderfully mended. Even he was obliged to admit that; but the scar was still visible to his keen eyes, a very fine line right across the face, downwards from right to left. Yet all the conditions had been most favourable for a cure, since the cement had set quite hard at the first attempt and the weather had been fine and dry, which makes a great difference in a dolls' hospital. At last he knew that he could do no more, and the under nurse had already come twice to see whether the job was finished, as she coarsely expressed it.

'Nina is not quite strong yet,' Mr Puckler had answered each time, for he could not make up his mind to face the parting.

And now he sat before the square deal table at which he worked, and Nina lay before him for the last time with a big brown-paper box beside her. It stood there like her coffin, waiting for her, he thought. He must put her into it, and lay tissue paper over her dear face, and then put on the lid, and at the thought of tying the string his sight was dim with tears again. He was never to look into the glassy depths of the beautiful brown eyes any more, nor to hear the little wooden voice say 'Pa-pa' and 'Ma-ma'. It was a very painful moment.

In the vain hope of gaining time before the separation, he took up the little sticky bottles of cement and glue and gum and colour, looking at each one in turn, and then at Nina's face. And all his small tools lay there, neatly arranged in a row, but he knew that he could not use them again for Nina. She was quite strong at last, and in a country where there should be no cruel children to hurt her she might live a hundred years, with only that almost imperceptible line across her face, to tell of the fearful thing that had befallen her on the marble steps of Cranston House.

Suddenly Mr Puckler's heart was quite full, and he rose abruptly from his seat and turned away.

'Else,' he said unsteadily, 'you must do it for me. I cannot bear to see her go into the box.'

So he went and stood at the window with his back turned, while Else did what he had not the heart to do.

'Is it done?' he asked, not turning round. 'Then take her away, my dear. Put on your hat, and take her to Cranston House quickly, and when you are gone I will turn round.'

Else was used to her father's queer ways with the dolls, and though she had never seen him so much moved by a parting, she was not much surprised.

'Come back quickly,' he said, when he heard her hand on the latch. 'It is growing late, and I should not send you at this hour. But I cannot bear to look forward to it any more.'

When Else was gone, he left the window and sat down in his place before the table again, to wait for the child to come back, He touched the place where Nina had lain, very gently, and he recalled the softly-tinted pink face, and the glass eyes, and the ringlets of yellow hair, till he could almost see them.

The evenings wore long, for it was late in the spring. But it began to grow dark soon, and Mr Puckler wondered why Else did not come back. She had been gone an hour and a half, and that was much longer than he had expected, for it was barely half a mile from Belgrave Square to Cranston House. He reflected that the child might have been kept waiting, but as the twilight deepened he grew anxious, and walked up and down in the dim workshop, no longer thinking of Nina, but of Else, his own living child, whom he loved.

An indefinable, disquieting sensation came upon him by fine degrees, a chilliness and a faint stirring of his thin hair, joined with a wish to be in any company rather than to be alone much longer. It was the beginning of fear.

He told himself in strong German-English that he was a foolish old man, and he began to feel about for the matches in the dusk. He knew just where they should be, for he always kept them in the same place, close to the little tin box that held bits of sealing wax of various colours, for some kinds of mending. But somehow he could not find the matches in the gloom.

Something had happened to Else, he was sure, and as his fear increased, he felt as though it might be allayed if he could get a light and see what time it was. Then he called himself a foolish old man again, and the sound of his own voice startled him in the dark. He could not find the matches.

The window was grey still; he might see what time it was if he went close to it, and he could go and get matches out of the cupboard afterwards. He stood back from the table, to get out of the way of the chair, and began to cross the board floor.

Something was following him in the dark. There was a small pattering, as of tiny feet upon the boards. He stopped and listened, and the roots of his hair tingled. It was nothing and he was a foolish old man. He made two steps more, and he was sure that he heard the little pattering again. He turned his back to the window, leaning against the sash so that the panes began to crack, and he faced the dark. Everything was quite still, and it smelt of paste and cement and wood-filings as usual.

'Is that you, Else?' he asked, and he was surprised by the fear in his voice.

There was no answer in the room, and he held up his watch and tried to make out what time it was by the grey dusk that was just not darkness. So far as he could see, it was within two or three minutes of ten o'clock. He had been a long time alone. He was shocked and frightened for Else, out in London, so late, and he almost ran across the room to the door. As he fumbled for the latch, he distinctly heard the running of the little feet after him.

'Mice!' he exclaimed feebly, just as he got the door open.

He shut it quickly behind him, and felt as though some cold thing had settled on his back and was writhing upon him. The passage was quite dark, but he found his hat and was out in the alley in a moment, breathing more freely, and surprised to find how much light there still was in the open air. He could see the pavement clearly under his feet, and far off in the street to which the alley led he could hear the laughter and calls of children, playing some game out of doors. He wondered how he could have been so nervous, and for an instant he thought of going back into the house to wait quietly for Else. But instantly he felt that nervous fright of something stealing over him again. In any case it was better to walk up to Cranston House and ask the servants about the child. One of the women had perhaps taken a fancy to her, and was even now giving her tea and cake.

He walked quickly to Belgrave Square, and then up the broad streets, listening as he went, whenever there was no other sound, for the tiny footsteps. But he heard nothing, and was laughing at himself when he rang the servants' bell at the big house. Of course, the child must be there.

The person who opened the door was quite an inferior person—for it was a back door—but affected the manners of the front, and stared at Mr Puckler superciliously.

No little girl had been seen, and he knew 'nothing about no dolls'.

'She is my little girl,' said Mr Puckler tremulously, for all his anxiety was returning tenfold, 'and I am afraid something has happened.'

The inferior person said rudely that 'nothing could have happened to her in that house, because she had not been there, which was a jolly good reason why'; and Mr Puckler was obliged to admit that the man ought to know, as it was his business to keep the door and let people in. He wished to be allowed to speak to the under nurse, who knew him; but the man was ruder than ever, and finally shut the door in his face.

When the doll doctor was alone in the street, he steadied himself by the railing, for he felt as though he were breaking in two, just as some dolls break, in the middle of the backbone.

Presently he knew that he must be doing something to find Else, and that gave him strength. He began to walk as quickly as he could through the streets, following every highway and byway which his little girl might have taken on her errand. He also asked several policemen in vain if they had seen her, and most of them answered him kindly, for they saw that he was a sober man and in his right senses, and some of them had little girls of their own.

It was one o'clock in the morning when he went up to his own door again, worn out and hopeless and broken-hearted. As he turned the key in the lock, his heart stood still, for he knew that he was awake and not dreaming, and that he really heard those tiny footsteps pattering to meet him inside the house along the passage.

But he was too unhappy to be much frightened anymore, and his heart went on again with a dull regular pain, that found its way all through him with every pulse. So he went in, and hung up his hat in the dark, and found the matches in the cupboard and the candlestick in its place in the corner. Mr Puckler was so much overcome and so completely worn out that he sat down in his chair before the work-table and almost fainted, as his face dropped forward upon his folded hands. Beside him the solitary candle burned steadily with a low flame in the still warm air.

'Else! Else!' he moaned against his yellow knuckles. And that was all he could say, and it was no relief to him. On the contrary, the very sound of the name was a new and sharp pain that pierced his ears and his head and his very soul. For every time he repeated the name it meant that little Else was dead, somewhere out in the streets of London in the dark.

He was so terribly hurt that he did not even feel something pulling gently at the skirt of his old coat, so gently that it was like the nibbling of a tiny mouse. He might have thought that it was really a mouse if he had noticed it.

'Else! Else!' he groaned, right against his hands.

Then a cool breath stirred his thin hair, and the low flame of the one candle dropped down almost to a mere spark, not flickering, as though a draught were going to blow it out, but just dropping down as if it were tired out. Mr Puckler felt his hands stiffening with fright under his face; and there was a faint rustling sound, like some small silk thing blown in a gentle breeze. He sat up straight, stark and scared, and a small wooden voice spoke in the stillness.

'Pa-pa,' it said, with a break between the syllables.

Mr Puckler stood up in a single jump, and his chair fell over backwards with a smashing noise upon the wooden floor. The candle had almost gone out.

It was Nina's doll-voice that had spoken, and he should have known it among the voices of a hundred other dolls. And yet there was something more in it, a little human ring, with a pitiful cry and a call for help, and the wail of a hurt child. Mr Puckler stood up, stark and stiff, and tried to look round, but at first he could not, for he seemed to be frozen from head to foot.

Then he made a great effort, and he raised one hand to each of his temples, and pressed his own head round as he would have turned a doll's. The candle was burning so low that it might as well have been out altogether, for any light it gave, and the room seemed quite dark at first. Then he saw something. He would not have believed that he could be more frightened than he had been just before that. But he was, and his knees shook, for he saw the doll standing in the middle of the floor, shining with a faint and ghostly radiance, her beautiful glassy brown eyes fixed on his. And across her face the very thin line of the break he had mended shone as though it were drawn in light with a line point of white flame.

Yet there was something more in the eyes, too; there was something human, like Else's own, but as if only the doll saw him through them, and not Else. And there was enough of Else to bring back all his pain and to make him forget his fear.

'Else! My little Else!' he cried aloud.

The small ghost moved, and its doll-arm slowly rose and fell with a stiff, mechanical motion.

'Pa-pa,' it said.

It seemed this time that there was even more of Else's tone echoing somewhere between the wooden notes that reached his ears so distinctly and yet so far away. Else was calling him, he was sure. His face was perfectly white in the gloom, but his knees did not shake any more, and he felt that he was less frightened.

'Yes, child! But where? Where?' he asked. 'Where are you, Else?'

'Pa-pa!'

The syllables died away in the quiet room.

There was a low rustling of silk, the glassy brown eyes turned slowly away, and Mr Puckler heard the pitter-patter of the small feet in the bronze kid slippers as the figure ran straight to the door. Then the candle burned high again, the room was full of light, and he was alone.

Mr Puckler passed his hand over his eyes and looked about him. He could see everything quite clearly, and he felt that he must have been dreaming, though he was standing instead of sitting down, as he should have been if he had just waked up. The candle burned brightly now. There were the dolls to be mended, lying in a row with their toes up. The third one had lost her right shoe, and Else was making one. He knew that, and he was certainly not dreaming now. He had not been dreaming when he had come in from his fruitless search and had heard the doll's footsteps running to the door. He had not fallen asleep in his chair. How could he possibly have fallen asleep when his heart was breaking? He had been awake all the time.

He steadied himself, set the fallen chair upon its legs, and said to himself again very emphatically that he was a foolish old man. He ought to be out in the streets looking for his child, asking questions, and enquiring at the police stations where all accidents were reported as soon as they were known, or at the hospitals.

'Pa-pa!'

The longing, wailing, pitiful little wooden cry rang from the passage, outside the door, and Mr Puckler stood for an instant with white face, transfixed and rooted to the spot. A moment later his hand was on the latch. Then he was in the passage, with the light streaming from the open door behind him.

Quite at the other end he saw the little phantom shining clearly in the shadow, and the right hand seemed to beckon to him as the arm rose and fell once more. He knew all at once that it had not come to frighten him but to lead him, and when it disappeared, and he walked boldly towards the door, he knew that it was in the street outside, waiting for him. He forgot that he was tired and had eaten no supper, and had walked many miles, for a sudden hope ran through and through him, like a golden stream of life.

And sure enough, at the corner of the alley, and at the corner of the street, and out in Belgrave Square, he saw the small ghost flitting before him. Sometimes it was only a shadow, where there was other light, but then the glare of the lamps made a pale green sheen on its little Mother Hubbard frock of silk; and sometimes, where the streets were dark and silent, the whole figure shone out brightly with its yellow curls and rosy neck. It seemed to trot along like a tiny child, and Mr Puckler could hear the pattering of the bronze kid slippers on the pavement as it ran. But it went very fast, and he could only just keep up with it, tearing along with his hat on the back of his head and his thin hair blown by the night breeze, and his horn-rimmed spectacles firmly set upon his broad nose.

On and on he went, and he had no idea where he was. He did not even care, for he knew certainly that he was going the right way.

Then at last, in a wide, quiet street, he was standing before a big, sober-looking door that had two lamps on each side of it, and a polished brass bell-handle, which he pulled.

And just inside, when the door was opened, in the bright light, there was the little shadow, and the pale green sheen of the little silk dress, and once more the small cry came to his ears, less pitiful, more longing.

'Pa-pa!'

The shadow turned suddenly bright, and out of the

brightness the beautiful brown glass eyes were turned up happily to his, while the rosy mouth smiled so divinely that the phantom doll looked almost like a little angel just then.

'A little girl was brought in soon after ten o'clock,' said the quiet voice of the hospital doorkeeper. 'I think they thought she was only stunned. She was holding a big brown-paper box against her, and they could not get it out of her arms. She had a long plait of brown hair that hung down as they carried her.'

'She is my little girl,' said Mr Puckler, but he hardly heard his own voice.

He leaned over Else's face in the gentle light of the children's ward, and when he had stood there a minute the beautiful brown eyes opened and looked up to his.

'Pa-pa!' cried Else softly, 'I knew you would come!'

Then Mr Puckler did not know what he did or said for a moment, and what he felt was worth all the fear and terror and despair that had almost killed him that night. But by and by Else was telling her story, and the nurse let her speak, for there were only two other children in the room, who were getting well and were sound asleep.

'They were big boys with bad faces,' said Else, 'and they tried to get Nina away from me, but I held on and fought as well as I could till one of them hit me with something, and I don't remember any more, for I tumbled down and I suppose the boys ran away, and somebody found me there. But I'm afraid Nina is all smashed.'

'Here is the box,' said the nurse. 'We could not take it out of her arms till she came to herself. Would you like to see if the doll is broken?'

And she undid the string cleverly, but Nina was all smashed to pieces. Only the gentle light of the children's ward made a pale green sheen in the folds of the little Mother Hubbard frock.

HAUNTED VILLAGES

Lt. Col. W.H. Sleeman

On the 16th, we came on nine miles to Amabe, the frontier village of the Jansee territory, bordering upon Duteea, where I had to receive the farewell visits of many members of the Jansee parties, who came on to have a quiet opportunity to assure me, that whatever may be the final order of the supreme government, they will do their best for the good of the people and the state, in whose welfare I feel great interest, for I have always considered Jansee among the native states of Bundelcund as a kind of oasis in the desert—the only one in which man can accumulate property with the confidence of being permitted by its rulers freely to display and enjoy it. I had also to receive the visit of messengers from the Rajah of Duteea, at whose capital we were to encamp the next day; and finally, to take leave of my amiable little friend the Sureemunt, who here left me on his return to Saugor, with a heavy heart I really believe.

We talked of the common belief among the agricultural classes, of villages being haunted by the spirits of ancient proprietors, whom it was thought necessary to propitiate. 'He knew,' he said, 'many instances where these spirits were so very froward, that the present heads of the villages which they haunted, and the members of their little communities, found it almost impossible to keep them in good humour; and their cattle and children were, in consequence, always liable to serious accidents of one kind or another. Sometimes they were bitten by snakes, sometimes became possessed by devils; and at others, were thrown down and beaten most unmercifully.' Any person who falls down in an epileptic fit is supposed to be thrown down by a ghost, or possessed by a devil. They feel little of our mysterious dread of ghosts—a sound drubbing is what they dread from them; and he who hurts himself in one of these fits is considered to have got it. 'As for himself, whenever he found any one of the villages upon his estate haunted by the spirit of an old Patel (village proprietor), he always made a point of giving him a neat little shrine; and having it well endowed and attended, to keep him in good humour: this he thought was a duty that every landlord owed to his tenants!' Ramchund, the pundit, said, 'Those villages which had been held by old Gond (mountaineer) proprietors were more liable than any other to those kinds of visitations—that it was easy to say what village was and was not haunted; but often exceedingly difficult to discover to whom the ghost belonged! This once discovered, his nearest surviving relation was, of course, expected to take steps to put him to rest; but,' said he, 'it is wrong to suppose that the ghost of an old proprietor must be always doing mischief—he is often the best friend of the cultivators, and of the present proprietor, too, if he treats him with proper respect; for he will not allow the people of any other village to encroach upon their boundaries with impunity; and they will be saved all the expense and annoyance of a reference to the Adawlut (judicial tribunals) for the settlement of boundary disputes. It will not cost much to conciliate these spirits; and the money is generally well laid out!'

Several anecdotes were told me in illustration; and all that I could urge against the probability or possibility of such visitations appeared to them very inconclusive and unsatisfactory; they mentioned the case of the family of village proprietors in the Saugor district, who had for several generations, at every new settlement, insisted upon having the name of the spirit of the old proprietor of another tribe inserted in the lease instead of their own, and thereby secured his good graces on all occasions. Mr Fraser had before mentioned this case to me. In August 1834, while engaged in the settlement of the land revenue of the Saugor district for twenty years, he was about to deliver the lease of the estate made out in due form to the head of the family, a very honest and respectable old gentleman, when he asked him, respectfully, in whose name it had been made out? 'In yours to be sure; have you renewed your lease for twenty years?' The old man, in a state of great alarm, begged him to have it altered immediately, or he and his family would all be destroyed—that the spirit of the ancient proprietor presided over the village community and its interests; and that all affairs of importance were transacted in his name. 'He is,' said the old man, 'a very jealous spirit; and will not admit of any living man being considered, for a moment, as a proprietor or joint proprietor of the estate! It has been held by me and my ancestors immediately under government for many generations; but the lease deeds have always been made out in his name; and ours have been inserted merely as his managers, or bailiffs—were this good old rule, under which we have so long prospered, to be now infringed, we should all perish under his anger.' Mr Fraser found, upon inquiry, that this had really been the case; and, to relieve the old man and his family from their fears, he had the papers made out afresh, and the *ghost* inserted as the proprietor! The modes of flattering and propitiating these beings, natural and supernatural, who are supposed to have the power to do mischief, are endless.

While I was in charge of the district of Nursingpore, in the valley of the Nerbudda, in 1823, a cultivator of the village of Bedoo, about twelve miles distant from my court, was one day engaged in the cultivation of his field on the border of the village of Burkhara, which was supposed to be haunted by the spirit of an old proprietor, whose temper was so froward and violent that the lands could hardly be let for anything; for hardly any man would venture to cultivate them lest he might unintentionally incur his ghostship's displeasure. The poor cultivator, after begging his pardon in secret, ventured to drive his plough a few yards beyond the proper line of his boundary, and thus to add half an acre of the lands of Burkhara to his own little tenement, which was situated in Bedoo. That very night his only son was bitten by a snake, and his two bullocks were seized with the murrain. In terror he went off to the village temple, confessed his sin, and vowed not only to restore the half acre of land to the village of Burkhara, but to build a very handsome shrine upon the spot as a perpetual sign of his repentance. The boy and the bullocks all three recovered, and the shrine was built; and is, I believe, still to be seen as the boundary mark!

The fact was that the village stood upon an elevated piece of ground rising out of a moist plain, and a colony of snakes had taken up their abode in it. The bites of these snakes had, on many occasions, proved fatal; and such accidents were all attributed to the anger of a spirit, which was supposed to haunt the village. At one time, under the former government, no one would take a lease of the village on any terms; and it had become almost entirely deserted, though the soil was the finest in the whole district. With a view to remove the whole prejudices of the people, the governor, Goroba Pundit, took the lease himself at the rent of one thousand rupees a year; and in the month of June went from his residence, twelve miles, with ten of his own ploughs, to superintend the commencement of so perilous an undertaking. On reaching the middle of the village, situated on the top of the little hill, he alighted from his horse, sat down upon a carpet that had been spread for him under a large and beautiful banyan tree, and began to refresh himself with a pipe before going to work in the fields. As he quaffed his hookah, and railed at the follies of men, 'whose absurd superstitions had made them desert so beautiful a village with so noble a tree in its centre,' his eyes fell upon an enormous black snake which had coiled round one of its branches immediately over his head, and seemed as if resolved at once to pounce down and punish him for his blasphemy! He gave his pipe to his attendant, mounted his horse, from which the saddle had not yet been taken, and never pulled rein till he got home. Nothing could ever induce him to visit this village again, though he was afterwards employed under me as a native collector; and he has often told me, that he verily believed this was the spirit of the old landlord that he had unhappily neglected to propitiate before taking possession!

My predecessor in the civil charge of that district, the late Mr Lindsay, of the Bengal civil service, again tried to remove the prejudices of the people against the occupation and cultivation of this fine village. It had never been measured; and all the revenue officers, backed by all the farmers and cultivators of the neighbourhood, declared that the spirit of the old proprietor would never allow it to be so. Mr Lindsay was a good geometrician, and had long been in the habit of superintending his revenue surveys himself; and on this occasion he thought himself particularly called upon to do so. A new measuring cord was made for the occasion, and with fear and trembling all his officers attended him to the first field; but in measuring it the rope, by some accident, broke! Poor Lindsay was that morning taken ill, and obliged to return to Nursingpore, where he died soon after from fever. No man was ever more beloved by all classes of the people of his district than he was; and I believe there was not one person among them who did not believe him to have fallen a victim to the resentment of the spirit of the old proprietor. When I went to the village some years afterwards, the people in the neighbourhood all declared to me, that they saw the cord with which he was measuring, fly into a thousand pieces the moment the men attempted to straighten it over the first field.

A very respectable old gentleman from the Concan, or Malabar coast, told me one day, that every man there protects his field of corn and his fruit tree by dedicating it to one or other of the spirits which there abound, or confiding it to his guardianship. He sticks up something in the field, or ties on something to the tree, in the name of the said spirit, who from that moment feels himself responsible for its safe-keeping. If anyone, without permission from the proprietor, presumes to take either an ear of corn from the field, or fruit from the tree, he is sure to be killed outright or made extremely ill. 'No other protection is required,' said the old gentleman, 'for our fields and fruit trees in that direction, though whole armies should have to march through them.' I once saw a man come to the proprietor of a jack tree, embrace his feet, and in the most piteous manner implore his protection. He asked what was the matter. 'I took,' said the man, 'a jack from your tree yonder three days ago, as I passed at night; and I have been suffering dreadful agony in my stomach ever since. The spirit of the tree is upon me, and you only can pacify him.' The proprietor took up a bit of cow dung, moistened it, and made a mark with it upon the man's forehead in the *name of the spirit*, and put some of it into the knot of hair on the top of his head. He had no sooner done this, than the man's pains all left him, and he went off, vowing never again to give similar cause of offence to one of these guardian spirits.'

'Men,' said my old friend, 'do not die there in the same regulated spirit, with their thoughts directed exclusively towards God, as in other parts; and whether a man's spirit is to haunt the world or not after his death all depends on that.'

A FACE IN THE DARK

Ruskin Bond

It may give you some idea of rural humour if I begin this tale with an anecdote that concerns me. I was walking alone through a village at night when I met an old man carrying a lantern. I found, to my surprise, that the man was blind. 'Old man,' I asked, 'if you cannot see, why do you carry a lamp?'

'I carry this,' he replied, 'so that fools do not stumble against me in the dark.'

This incident has only a slight connection with the story that follows, but I think it provides the right sort of tone and setting. Mr Oliver, an Anglo-Indian teacher, was returning to his school late one night, on the outskirts of the hill-station of Simla. The school was conducted on English public school lines and the boys, most of them from well-to-do Indian families, wore blazers, caps and ties. *Life* magazine, in a feature on India had once called this school the 'Eton of the East'.

Individuality was not encouraged; they were all destined to become 'leaders of men'.

Mr Oliver had been teaching in the school for several years. Sometimes it seemed like an eternity; for one day followed another with the same monotonous routine. The Simla bazaar, with its cinemas and restaurants, was about two miles from the school; and Mr Oliver, a bachelor, usually strolled into the town in the evening, returning after dark, when he would take a short cut through a pine forest.

When there was a strong wind, the pine trees made sad, eerie sounds that kept most people to the main road. But Mr Oliver was not a nervous or imaginative man. He carried a torch and, on the night I write of, its pale gleam—the batteries were running down—moved fitfully over the narrow forest path. When its flickering light fell on the figure of a boy, who was sitting alone on a rock, Mr Oliver stopped. Boys were not supposed to be out of school after 7 p.m., and it was now well past nine.

'What are you doing out here, boy?' asked Mr Oliver sharply, moving closer so that he could recognize the miscreant. But even as he approached the boy, Mr Oliver sensed that something was wrong. The boy appeared to be crying. His head hung down, he held his face in his hands, and his body shook convulsively. It was a strange, soundless weeping, and Mr Oliver felt distinctly uneasy.

'Well—what's the matter?' he asked, his anger giving way to concern. 'What are you crying for?' The boy would not answer or look up. His body continued to be racked with silent sobbing.

'Come on, boy, you shouldn't be out here at this hour. Tell me the trouble. Look up!'

The boy looked up. He took his hands from his face and looked up at his teacher. The light from Mr Oliver's torch fell on the boy's face—if you could call it a face.

He had no eyes, ears, nose, or mouth. It was just a round, smooth head—with a school cap on top of it. And that's where the story should end—as indeed it has for several people who have had similar experiences and dropped dead of inexplicable heart attacks. But for Mr Oliver it did not end there.

The torch fell from his trembling hand. He turned and scrambled down the path, running blindly through the trees and calling for help. He was still running towards the school building when he saw a lantern swinging in the middle of the path. Mr Oliver had never before been so pleased to see the night-watchman. He stumbled up to the watchman, gasping for breath and speaking incoherently.

'What is it, Sir?' asked the watchman. 'Has there been an accident? Why are you running?'

'I saw something—something horrible—a boy weeping in the forest—and he had no face!'

'No face, Sir?'

'No eyes, nose, mouth—nothing.'

'Do you mean it was like this, Sir?' asked the watchman, and raised the lamp to his own face. The watchman had no eyes, no ears, no features at all—not even an eyebrow!

The wind blew the lamp out, and Mr Oliver had his heart attack.

A WORM'S TURNING

John Eyton

He was a nameless hill labourer—a natural slave if ever there was one. He was utterly out of keeping with these days of Labour Unions and limited hours and representative government—an anachronism, a survival of the days when men were herded and driven. It was such as he who laboured in old-time quarries, and drove galleys, and piled the pyramids. So he was out of his time, a blot on the landscape, and a mockery at the beneficent government which professed such high care for the untutored masses of India. Yet he was not alone; he toiled with hundreds of his kind—men and women—along the mountain way leading to Bhawali. He was a carrier of woods; Heaven knows how many times a day his task was to carry a great solid block of Sal wood—six feet by one foot six by six inches, or something like it—for a mile and a half up the hot, dusty path.

He was only familiar to me because he was older than the rest. His face was seamed and lined, and his hair grey. He carried his solid block of wood on his back, length ways; a rope passed across his forehead—which was bound with a dirty cloth—and another rope under his arms. He lived stooping forwards. The weight was obviously as much as he could stand; he was just able to put one foot before the other, and the muscles of his calves and thighs always trembled. He looked perpetually on the ground, with eyes that started a little out of his head staring. They had no expression, save of intense strain. They saw nothing, noted nothing. They were the eyes of an animal—or of a slave.

Sweat poured from his face and limbs, for all that he wore only a little wisp of dingy cloth round his waist and loins. It was obviously a tremendous effort to him to move out of the path for a rider to pass. When he did, it was with the stumbling, tottering gait of a blind beast of burden.

When he rested for a few minutes, he still could not escape his plank: he had to stand upright, with the plank resting against the wall of rock at the roadside. His face on these occasions showed utter weariness—the other men talked and laughed; but with him it was as if life had been squeezed out, leaving but a blind automaton. He would rest in silence—then get up and plod wearily on.

He had a little time off for food; otherwise he did a full day's work that a beast would have done in the plains, and that a rope railway might have done years ago in the hills. He had no encouragement; there was no question of efficiency or dispatch; pay was according to the weight carried on each journey, and the sole standard of ability was weight-carrying capacity. There was no pension for long service; he and his kind carried wood—or heavy cases or pianos, as the case might be—until they dropped. At night he must have slept the sleep of a worn-out beast. If he thought at all, he must have been haunted by the fear—'One day I shall not be able to get up with the wood when they load me. The babu will send me away.' Then release—utter poverty—death. He could hardly have escaped that thought—he was so clearly past the work.

I knew the babu by sight; he was the pay-clerk of the local contractor to the Forest Department. I have reason to believe that he took his toll of the labourers—a small commission for employment; perhaps an anna in the rupee; only 6 per cent. His name was Debi Datt—a tall, weedy specimen, who affected English dress and perched his little cap jauntily on the side of his head. He had a black moustache, shifty brown eyes, thick lips, and no chin. He walked about with the swagger of a cavalryman and the assurance of a millionaire—but you could have blown him over easily enough. I also know that he had run through a number of clerkships in various offices, earning the encomiums of 'incorrigibly lazy', 'insufferably idle', 'utterly untrustworthy', and so on. The forest contractor had taken him on because he was his nephew, and cheap. The latter word aptly describes him.

I did not see the finale between the babu and the man, but I heard the account of an eyewitness.

It happened on the hottest day of the year in the hills— just before the rains. Debi Datt was dispatching—telling off the men's burdens, weighing them, and noting them in his little book. The labourers moved slowly off in parties of six. The weighing was done at a point where the mountain path broadened to a width of seven or eight yards, thus giving room for a clearing station. Below, as usual, there was a steep khud—a sheer drop of fifty feet.

The turn of the old man came, and he moved forward for his burden to be adjusted. It was a particularly massive piece of timber; an ordinary person would have found it difficult to raise one end of it off the ground. The old man murmured something, to which the babu replied roughly. The timber was duly adjusted; the order was given—'Chalo!' The old man strained to raise himself, but failed. He looked round at the babu with a world of pathos in his eyes, as if to say 'You have me beaten at last.' The look was that of an animal—asking for nothing, hoping for nothing—accepting fate. But he did not give up. Again and again he strained, groaning at the weight. At last he really did almost stand up—his joints cracking—then collapsed again.

It was then that the babu kicked him—once, twice, in the ribs with his pointed shoe. There was a grunt of pain, like a sob, and then the unique thing happened. Without an alteration of expression, but with a gigantic heave of the whole body, the old man was on his feet. He stood for the slightest instant, feeling his balance, and then swung sharply round. The whole weight of the butt of timber struck the babu, sweeping him back, spinning him over the khud.

Then the old man overbalanced and followed him, the timber bumping against the rocks. There were two dull thuds a long way below... No worm had ever turned more effectively.

CORONER'S INQUEST

Marc Connelly

'What is your name?'

'Frank Wineguard.'

'Where do you live?'

A hundred and eighty-five West Fifty-fifth Street.'

'What is your business?'

'I'm stage manager for *Hello, America.*'

'You were the employer of James Dawle?'

'In a way. We both worked for Mr Bender, the producer, but I have charge backstage.'

'Did you know Theodore Rebel?'

'Yes, sir.'

'Was he in your company, too?'

'No, sir. I met him when we started rehearsals. That was about three months ago, in June. We sent out a call for midgets and he and Jimmy showed up together, with a lot of others. Robel was too big for us. I didn't see him again until we broke into their room Tuesday.'

'You discovered their bodies?'

'Yes, sir. Mrs Pike, there, was with me.'

'You found them both dead?'

'Yes, sir.'

'How did you happen to be over in Jersey City?'

'Well, I called up his house at curtain time Monday night when I found Jimmy hadn't shown up for the performance. Mrs Pike told me they were both out, and I asked her to have either Jimmy or Robel call me when they came in. Then Mrs Pike called me Tuesday morning and said she tried to get into the room but she'd found the door was bolted. She said all her other roomers were out and she was alone and scared.'

'I'd kind of suspected something might be wrong. So I said to her to wait and I'd come over. Then I took the tube over and got there about noon. Then we went up and I broke down the door.'

'Did you see this knife there?'

'Yes, sir. It was on the floor, about a foot from Jimmy.'

'You say you suspected something was wrong. What do you mean by that?'

'I mean I felt something might have happened to Jimmy. Nothing like this, of course. But I knew he'd been feeling very depressed lately, and I knew Robel wasn't helping to cheer him up any.'

'You mean that they had quarrels?'

'No, sir. They just both had the blues. Robel had them for a long time. Robel was Jimmy's brother-in-law. He'd married Jimmy's sister—she was a midget, too—about five years ago, but she died a year or so later. Jimmy had been living with them and after the sister died, he and Robel took a room in Mrs Pike's house together.'

'How did you learn this?'

'Jimmy and I were pretty friendly at the theatre. He was a nice little fellow and seemed grateful that I'd given him this job. We'd only needed one midget for an Oriental scene in the second act and the agencies had sent about fifteen. Mr Gehring, the director, told me to pick one of them as he was busy and I picked Jimmy because he was the littlest.

'After I got to know him he told me how glad he was I'd given him the job. He hadn't worked for nearly a year. He wasn't little enough to be a featured midget with circuses or in museums, so he had to take whatever came along. Anyway, we got to be friendly and he used to tell me about his brother-in-law and all.'

'He never suggested that there might be ill-feeling between him and his brother-in-law?'

'No, sir. I don't imagine he'd ever had any words at all with Robel. As a matter of fact, from what I could gather I guess Jimmy had quite a lot of affection for him and he certainly did everything he could to help him. Robel was a lot worse off than Jimmy. Robel hadn't worked for a couple of years and Jimmy practically supported him. He used to tell me how Robel had been sunk ever since he got his late growth.'

'His, what?'

'His late growth. I heard it happens among midgets often, but Jimmy told me about it first. Usually a midget will stay as long as he lives at whatever height he reaches when he's fourteen or fifteen, but every now and then one of them starts growing again just before he's thirty, and he can grow a foot or even more in a couple of years. Then he stops growing for good. But, of course, he don't look so much like a midget any more.'

'That's what had happened to Robel about three years ago. Of course he had trouble getting jobs and it hit him pretty hard.

'From what Jimmy told me and from what Mrs Pike says, I guess he used to talk about it all the time. Robel used to come over and see his agent in New York twice a week, but there was never anything for him. Then he'd go back to Jersey City.

Most of the week he lived alone because after the show started Jimmy often stayed in New York with a cousin or somebody that lived uptown.

'Lately Robel hadn't been coming over to New York at all. But every Saturday night Jimmy would go over to Jersey City and stay till Monday with him, trying to cheer him up. Every Sunday they'd take a walk and go to a movie. I guess as they walked along the street Robel realized most the difference in their heights. And I guess that's really why they're both dead now.'

'How do you mean?'

'Well, as I told you, Jimmy would try to sympathize with Robel and cheer him up. He and Robel both realized that Jimmy was working and supporting them and that Jimmy would probably keep right on working, according to the ordinary breaks of the game, while Robel would always be too big. It simply preyed on Robel's mind.

'And then three weeks ago on a Monday Jimmy thought he saw the axe fall.

'I was standing outside the stage door—it was about seven-thirty—and Jimmy came down the alley. He looked down in the mouth, which I thought was strange, seeing that he usually used to come in swinging his little cane and looking pretty cheerful. I said, "How are you feeling, Jimmy?" and he said, "I don't feel so good, Mr Wineguard." So I said, "Why, what's the matter, Jimmy?" I could see there really was something the matter with him by this time.

'"I'm getting scared," he said, and I said, "Why?"

'"I'm starting to grow again," he says. He said it the way you just found out you had some disease that was going to kill you in a week. He looked like he was shivering.

'"Why, you're crazy, Jimmy," I says. "You ain't growing."

'"Yes, I am," he says. "I'm thrity-one and it's that late growth like my brother-in-law has. My father had it, but his people had money, so it didn't make much difference to him. It's different with me. I've got to keep working."

'He went on like that for a while and then I tried to kid him out of it.

'"You look all right to me," I said. "How tall have you been all along?"

'"Thirty-seven inches," he says. So I says, "Come on into the prop-room and I'll measure you."

'He backed away from me. "No," he says, "I don't want to know how much it is." Then he went up to the dressing-room before I could argue with him.

'All week he looked awful sunk. When he showed up the next Monday evening he looked almost white.

'I grabbed him as he was starting upstairs to make-up.

'"Come on out of it," I says. I thought he'd make a break and try to get away from me, but he didn't. He just sort of smiled as if I didn't understand. Finally, he says, "It ain't any use, Mr Wineguard."

'"Listen," I says, "you've been over with that brother-in-law of yours, haven't you?" he said yes, he had. "Well," I says, "that's what's bothering you. From what you tell me about him he's talked about his own tough luck so much that he's given you the willies, too. Stay away from him the end of this week."

'He stood there for a second without saying anything. They he says, "That wouldn't do any good. He's all alone over there and he needs company. Anyway, it's all up with me, I guess. I've grown nearly two inches already."

'I looked at him. He was pretty pathetic, but outside of that there wasn't any change in him as far as I could see.

'I says, "Have you been measured?" he said he hadn't. Then

I said, "Then how do you know? Your clothes fit you all right, except your pants, and as a matter of fact they seem a little longer."

"'I fixed my suspenders and let them down a lot farther," he says. "Besides they were always a little big for me."

"'Let's make sure," I says. "I'll get a yardstick and we'll make absolutely sure."

'But I guess he was too scared to face things. He wouldn't do it.

'He managed to dodge me all week. Then, last Saturday night, I ran into him as I was leaving the theatre. I asked him if he felt any better.

"'I feel all right," he says. He really looked scared to death.

'That's the last time I saw him before I went over to Jersey City after Mrs Pike phoned me Tuseday morning.'

'Patrolman Gorlitz has testified that the bodies were in opposite ends of the room when he arrived. They were in that position when you forced open the door?'

'Yes, sir.'

'The medical examiner has testified that they were both dead of knife wounds, apparently from the same knife. Would you assume the knife had fallen from Dawle's hand as he fell?'

'Yes, sir.'

'Has it been your purpose to suggest that both men were driven to despondency by a fear of lack of employment for Dawle, and that they might have committed suicide?'

'No, sir. I don't think anything of the kind.'

'What do you mean?'

'Well, when Mrs Pike and I went in the room and I got a look at the knife, I said to Mrs Pike that that was a funny kind of a knife for them to have in the room. You can see it's a kind of a butcher knife. Then Mrs Pike told me it was one that she'd missed from her kitchen a few weeks before. She'd never thought either Robel or Jimmy had stolen it, too. Then I put two and two together and found out what really happened. Have you got the little broken cane that was lying on the bed?'

'Is this it?'

'Yes, sir. Well, I'd never been convinced by Jimmy that he was really growing. So when Mrs Pike told me about the knife I started figuring. I figured that about five minutes before that knife came into play Jimmy must have found it, probably by accident.'

'Why by accident?'

'Because Robel had gone a little crazy, I guess. He'd stolen it and kept it hidden from Jimmy. And when Jimmy found it he wondered what Robel had been doing with it. Then Robel wouldn't tell him and Jimmy found out for himself. Or maybe Robel did tell him. Anyway, Jimmy looked at the cane. It was the one he always carried. He saw where, when Jimmy wasn't looking, Robel had been cutting little pieces off the end of it.

THE DECOY

Algernon Blackwood

It belonged to the category of unlovely houses about which an ugly superstition clings, one reason being, perhaps, its inability to inspire interest in itself without assistance. It seemed too ordinary to possess individuality, much less to exert an influence. Solid and ungainly, its huge bulk dwarfing the park timber, its best claim to notice was a negative one—it was unpretentious.

From the little hill its expressionless windows stared across the Kentish Weald, indifferent to weather, dreary in winter, bleak in spring, unblessed in summer. Some colossal hand had tossed it down, then let it starve to death, a country mansion that might well strain the adjectives of advertisers and find inheritors with difficulty. Its soul had fled, said some; it had committed suicide, thought others; and it was an inheritor, before he killed himself in the library, who thought this latter, yielding, apparently, to a hereditary taint in the family. For two other inheritors followed suit, with an interval of twenty years between them, and there was no clear reason to explain the three disasters. Only the first owner, indeed, lived permanently in the house, the others using it in the summer months and then deserting it with relief. Hence, when John Burley, present inheritor, assumed possession, he entered a house about which clung an ugly superstition, based, nevertheless, upon a series of undeniably ugly facts.

This century deals harshly with superstitious folk, deeming them fools or charlatans; but John Burley, robust, contemptuous of half lights, did not deal harshly with them, because he did not deal with them at all. He was hardly aware of their existence. He ignored them as he ignored, say, the Esquimaux, poets, and other human aspects that did not touch his scheme of life. A successful businessman, he concentrated on what was real; he dealt with business people. His philanthropy, on a big scale, was also real; yet, though he would have denied it vehemently, he had his superstition as well. No man exists without some taint of superstition in his blood; the racial heritage is too rich to be escaped entirely. Burley's took this form—that unless he gave his tithe to the poor he would not prosper. This ugly mansion, he decided, would make an ideal Convalescent Home.

'Only cowards or lunatics kill themselves,' he declared flatly, when his use of the house was criticized. 'I'm neither one nor t'other.' He let out his gusty, boisterous laugh. In his invigorating atmosphere such weakness seemed contemptible, just as superstition in his presence seemed the feeblest ignorance. Even its picturesqueness faded. 'I can't conceive,' he boomed, 'can't even imagine to myself,' he added emphatically, 'the state of mind in which a man can *think* of suicide, much less do it.' He threw his chest out with a challenging air. 'I tell you, Nancy, it's either cowardice or mania. And I've no use for either.'

Yet he was easy-going and good-humoured in his denunciation. He admitted his limitations with a hearty laugh which his wife called noisy. Thus he made allowances for the fairy fears of sailorfolk, and had even been known to mention haunted ships his companies owned. But he did so in the terms of tonnage and £ s.d. His scope was big; details were made for clerks.

His consent to pass a night in the mansion was the consent of a practical businessman and philanthropist who dealt condescendingly with foolish human nature. It was based on the commonsense of tonnage and £ s.d. The local newspapers had revived the silly story of the suicides, calling attention to the effect of the superstition upon the fortunes of the house, and so, possibly, upon the fortunes of its present owner. But the mansion, otherwise a white elephant, was precisely ideal for his purpose, and so trivial a matter as spending a night in it should not stand in the way. 'We must take people as we find them, Nancy.'

His young wife had her motive, of course, in making the proposal, and, if she was amused by what she called 'spook-hunting', he saw no reason to refuse her the indulgence. He loved her, and took her as he found her—late in life. To allay the superstitions of prospective staff and patients and supporters, all, in fact, whose goodwill was necessary to success, he faced this boredom of a night in the building before its opening was announced. 'You see, John, if you, the owner, do this, it will nip damaging talk in the bud. If anything went wrong later it would only be put down to this suicide idea, this haunting influence. The home will have a bad name from the start. There'll be endless trouble. It will be a failure.'

'You think my spending a night there will stop the nonsense?' he enquired.

'According to the old legend it breaks the spell,' she replied. 'That's the condition, anyhow.'

'But somebody's sure to die there sooner or later,' he objected.

'We can't prevent that. We can prevent people whispering

that they died unnaturally.' She explained the working of the public mind.

'I see,' he replied, his lip curling, yet quick to gauge the truth of what she told him about collective instinct.

'Unless *you* take poison in the hall,' she added laughingly, 'or elect to hang yourself with your braces from the hat peg.'

'I'll do it,' he agreed, after a moment's thought. 'I'll sit up with you. It will be like a honeymoon over again, you and I on the spree—eh?' He was even interested now; the boyish side of him was touched perhaps; but his enthusiasm was less when she explained that three was a better number than two on such an expedition.

'I've often done it before, John. We were always three.'

'Who?' he asked bluntly. He looked wonderingly at her, but she answered that if anything went wrong a party of three provided a better margin for help. It was sufficiently obvious. He listened and agreed. 'I'll get young Mortimer,' he suggested. 'Will he do?'

She hesitated. 'Well—he's cheery; he'll be interested, too. Yes, he's as good as another.' She seemed indifferent.

'And he'll make the time pass with his stories,' added her husband.

So Captain Mortimer, late officer on a T.B.D., a 'cheery lad', afraid of nothing, cousin of Mrs Burley, and now filling a good post in the company's London offices, was engaged as third hand in the expedition. But Captain Mortimer was young and ardent, and Mrs Burley was young and pretty and ill-mated, and John Burley was a neglectful and self-satisfied husband.

Fate laid the trap with cunning, and John Burley, blind-eyed, careless of detail, floundered into it. He also floundered out again, though in a fashion none could have expected of him.

The night agreed upon eventually was as near to the shortest in the year as John Burley could contrive—18 June—when the sun set at 8.18 and rose about a quarter to four. There would be barely three hours of true darkness. 'You're the expert,' he admitted, as she explained that only sitting through the actual darkness was required, not necessarily from sunset to sunrise. 'We'll do the thing properly. Mortimer's not very keen, he had a dance or something,' he added, noticing the look of annoyance that flashed swiftly in her eyes, 'but he got out of it. He's coming.' The pouting expression of the spoilt woman amused him. 'Oh, no, he didn't need much persuading really,' he assured her. 'Some girl or other, of course. He's young, remember.' To which no comment was forthcoming, though the implied comparison made her flush.

They motored from South Audley Street after an early tea, in due course passing Sevenoaks and entering the Kentish Weald; and, in order that the necessary advertisement be given, the chauffeur, warned strictly to keep their purpose quiet, was to put up at the country inn and fetch them an hour after sunrise; they would breakfast in London. 'He'll tell everybody,' said his practical and cynical master; 'the local newspaper will have it all next day. A few hours' discomfort is worthwhile if it ends the nonsense. We'll read and smoke, and Mortimer shall tell us yarns about the sea.' He went with the driver into the house to superintend the arrangement of the room, the lights, the hampers of food, and so forth, leaving the pair upon the lawn.

'Four hours isn't much, but it's something,' whispered Mortimer, alone with her for the first time since they started. 'It's simply ripping of you to have got me in. You look divine tonight. You're the most wonderful woman in the world.' His blue eyes shone with the hungry desire he mistook for love. He looked as if he had blown in from the sea, for his skin was tanned and his light hair bleached a little by the sun. He took her hand, drawing her out of the slanting sunlight towards the rhododendrons.

'I didn't, you silly boy. It was John who suggested your coming.' She released her hand with an affected effort. 'Besides, you overdid it—pretending you had a dance.'

'You could have objected,' he said eagerly, 'and didn't. Oh, you're too lovely, you're delicious!' He kissed her suddenly with passion. There was a tiny struggle, in which she yielded too easily, he thought.

'Harry, you're an idiot!' she cried breathlessly, when he let her go. 'I really don't know how you dare! And John's your friend. Besides, you know'—she glanced round quickly— 'it isn't safe here.' Her eyes shone happily, her cheeks were flaming. She looked what she was—a pretty, young, lustful animal, false to ideals, true to selfish passion only. 'Luckily,' she added, 'he trusts me too fully to think anything.'

The young man, worship in his eyes, laughed gaily. 'There's no harm in a kiss,' he said. 'You're a child to him, he never thinks of you as a woman. Anyhow, his head's full of ships and kings and scaling-wax,' he comforted her, while respecting her sudden instinct which warned him not to touch her again, 'and he never sees anything. Why, even at ten yards—'

From twenty yards away a big voice interrupted him, as John Burley came round a corner of the house and across the lawn towards them. The chauffeur, he announced, had left the hampers in the room on the first floor and gone back to the inn. 'Let's take a walk round,' he added, joining them, 'and see the garden. Five minutes before sunset we'll go in and feed.' He laughed. 'We must do the thing faithfully, you know, mustn't we, Nancy? Dark to dark, remember. Come on, Mortimer'—he took the young man's arm—'a last look round before we go in and hang ourselves from adjoining hooks in the matron's room!'

He reached out his free hand towards his wife.

'Oh, hush, John!' she said quickly. 'I don't like—especially now the dusk is coming.' She shivered, as though it were a genuine little shiver, pursing her lips deliciously as she did so; whereupon he drew her forcibly to him, saying he was sorry, and kissed her exactly where she had been kissed two minutes before, while young Mortimer looked on. 'We'll take care of you between us,' he said. Behind a broad back the pair exchanged a swift but meaning glance, for there was that in his tone which enjoined wariness, and perhaps after all he was not so blind as he appeared. They had their code, these two. 'All's well,' was signalled; 'but another time be more careful!'

There still remained some minutes' sunlight before the huge red ball of fire would sink behind the wooded hills, and the trio, talking idly, a flutter of excitement to two hearts certainly, walked among the roses. It was a perfect evening, windless, perfumed, warm. Headless shadows preceded them gigantically across the lawn as they moved, and one side of the great building lay already dark; bats were flitting, moths darted to and fro above the azalea and rhododendron clumps. The talk turned chiefly on the uses of the mansion as a Convalescent Home, its probable running cost, suitable staff, and so forth.

'Come along,' John Burley said presently, breaking off and turning abruptly, 'we must be inside, actually inside, before the sun's gone. We must fulfil the conditions faithfully,' he repeated as though fond of the phrase. He was in earnest over everything in life, big or little, once he set his hand to it.

They entered, this incongruous trio of ghost-hunters, not one of them really intent upon the business in hand, and went slowly upstairs to the great room where the hampers lay. Already in the hall it was dark enough for three electric torches to flash usefully and help their steps as they moved with caution, lighting one corner after another. The air inside was chill and damp. 'Like an unused museum,' said Mortimer. 'I can smell the specimens.' They looked about them, sniffing.

'That's humanity,' declared his host, employer, friend, 'with cement and whitewash to flavour it'; and all three laughed as Mrs Burley said she wished they had picked some roses and brought them in. Her husband was again in front on the broad staircase, Mortimer just behind him, when she called out.

'I don't like being last,' she exclaimed. 'It's so black behind me in the hall. I'll come between you two,' and the sailor took her outstretched hand, squeezing it, as he passed her up. 'There's a figure, remember,' she said hurriedly turning to gain her husband's attention, as when she touched wood at home. 'A figure is seen; that's part of the story. The figure of a man.' She gave a tiny shiver of pleasure, half-imagined alarm as she took his arm.

'I hope we shall see it,' he mentioned prosaically.

'I hope we shan't,' she replied with emphasis. 'It's only seen before—something happens.' Her husband said nothing, while Mortimer remarked facetiously that it would be a pity if they had their trouble for nothing.

'Something can hardly happen to all three of us,' he said lightly, as they entered a large room where the paper-hangers had conveniently left a rough table of bare planks. Mrs Burley, busy with her own thoughts, began to unpack the sandwiches and wine. Her husband strolled over to the window. He seemed restless.

'So this'—his deep voice startled her—'is where one of us'— he looked round him—'is to—'

'John!' She stopped him sharply, with impatience. 'Several times already I've begged you.' Her voice rang rather shrill and querulous in the empty room, a new note in it. She was beginning to feel the atmosphere of the place, perhaps. On the sunny lawn it had not touched her, but now, with the fall of night, she was aware of it, as shadow called to shadow and the kingdom of darkness gathered power. Like a great whispering gallery, the whole house listened.

'Upon my word, Nancy,' he said with contrition, as he came and sat down beside her, 'I quite forgot again. Only I cannot take it seriously. It's utterly unthinkable to me that a man—'

'But why evoke the idea at all?' she insisted in a lowered voice, that snapped despite its faintness. 'Men, after all, don't do such things for nothing.'

'We don't know everything in the universe, do we?' Mortimer put in, trying clumsily to support her. 'All I know just now is that I'm famished and this veal and ham pie is delicious.' He was very busy with his knife and fork. His foot rested lightly on her own beneath the table; he could not keep his eyes off her face; he was continually passing new edibles to her.

'No,' agreed John Burley, 'not everything. You're right there.'

She kicked the younger man gently, flashing a warning with her eyes as well, while her husband, emptying his glass, his head thrown back, looked straight at them over the rim, apparently seeing nothing. They smoked their cigarettes round the table, Burley lighting a big cigar. 'Tell us about the figure, Nancy?' he inquired. 'At least there's no harm in that. It's new to me. I hadn't heard about a figure.' And she did so willingly, turning her chair sideways from the dangerous, reckless feet. Mortimer could now no longer touch her.

'I know very little,' she confessed; 'only what the paper said. It's a man and he changes.'

'How changes?' asked her husband. 'Clothes, you mean, or what?'

Mrs Burley laughed, as though she was glad to laugh. Then

she answered: 'According to the story he shows himself each time to the man—'

'The man who—?'

'Yes, yes, of course. He appears to the man who dies—as himself.'

'H'm,' grunted her husband, naturally puzzled. He stared at her.

'Each time the chap saw his own double'—Mortimer came this time usefully to the rescue—'before he did it.'

Considerable explanation followed, involving much psychic jargon from Mrs Burley, which fascinated and impressed the sailor, who thought her as wonderful as she was lovely, showing it in his eyes for all to see. John Burley's attention wandered. He moved over to the window, leaving them to finish the discussion between them; he took no part in it, made no comment even, merely listening idly and watching them with an air of absent-mindedness through the cloud of cigar smoke round his head. He moved from window to window, ensconcing himself in turn in each deep embrasure, examining the fastenings, measuring the thickness of the stonework with his handkerchief. He seemed restless, bored, obviously out of place in this ridiculous expedition. On his big massive face lay a quiet, resigned expression his wife had never seen before. She noticed it now as the discussion ended, and the pair tidied away the debris of dinner, lit the spirit lamp for coffee and laid out a supper which would be very welcome with the dawn. A draught passed through the room, making the papers flutter on the table. Mortimer turned down the smoking lamps with care.

'Wind's getting up a bit—from the south,' observed Burley from his niche, closing one-half of the casement window as he said it. To do this, he turned his back a moment, fumbling for several seconds with the latch, while Mortimer, noting it, seized his sudden opportunity with the foolish abandon of his age and temperament. Neither he nor his victim perceived that, against the outside darkness, the interior of the room was plainly reflected in the window-pane. One reckless, the other terrified, they snatched the fearful joy, which might, after all, have been lengthened by another full half-minute, for the head they feared, followed by the shoulders, pushed through the side of the casement still open, and remained outside, taking in the night.

'A grand air,' said his deep voice, as the head drew in again. 'I'd like to be at sea a night like this.' He left the casement open and came across the room towards them. 'Now,' he said cheerfully, arranging a seat for himself, 'let's get comfortable for the night. Mortimer, we expect stories from you without ceasing, until dawn or the ghost arrives. Horrible stories of chains and headless men, remember. Make it a night we shan't forget in a hurry.' He produced his gust of laughter.

They arranged their chairs, with other chairs to put their feet on, and Mortimer contrived a footstool by means of a hamper for the smallest feet; the air grew thick with tobacco smoke; eyes flashed and answered, watched perhaps as well; ears listened and perhaps grew wise; occasionally, as a window shook, they started and looked around; there were sounds about the house from time to time, when the entering wind, using broken or open windows, set loose objects rattling.

But Mrs Burley vetoed horrible stories with decision. A big, empty mansion, lonely in the country, and even with the comfort of John Burley and a lover in it, has its atmosphere. Furnished rooms are far less ghostly. This atmosphere now came creeping everywhere, through spacious halls and sighing corridors, silent, invisible, but all-pervading, John Burley alone impervious to it, unaware of its soft attack upon the nerves. It entered possibly with the summer night wind, but possibly it was always there and Mrs Burley looked often at her husband, sitting near her at an angle; the light fell on his fine strong face; she felt that, though apparently so calm and quiet, he was really very restless; something about him was a little different; she could not define it; his mouth seemed set as with an effort; he looked, she thought curiously to herself, patient and very dignified; he was rather a dear after all. Why did she think the face inscrutable? Her thoughts wandered vaguely, unease, discomfort among them somewhere, while the heated blood—she had taken her share of wine—seethed in her.

Burley turned to the sailor for more stories. 'Sea and wind in them,' he asked. 'No horrors, remember!' And Mortimer told a tale about the shortage of rooms at a Welsh seaside place where spare rooms fetched fabulous prices, and one man alone refused to let—a retired captain of South Seas trader, very poor, a bit crazy apparently. He had two furnished rooms in his house worth twenty guineas a week. The rooms faced south; he kept them full of flowers; but he would not let. An explanation of his unworldly obstinacy was not forthcoming until Mortimer—they fished together—gained his confidence. 'The South Wind lives in them,' the old fellow told him. 'I keep them free for her.'

'For *her*?'

'It was on the South Wind my love came to me,' said the other softly; 'and it was on the South Wind that she felt—'

It was an odd tale to tell in such company, but he told it well.

'Beautiful,' thought Mrs Burley. Aloud she said a quiet, 'Thank you. By 'left' I suppose he meant she died or ran away?'

John Burley looked up with a certain surprise. 'We ask for a story,' he said, 'and you give us a poem.' He laughed. 'You're in love, Mortimer,' he informed him, 'and with my wife, probably.'

'Of course I am, sir,' replied the young man gallantly. 'A

sailor's heart, you know,' while the face of the woman turned pink, then white. She knew her husband more intimately than Mortimer did, and there was something in his tone, his eyes, his words, she did not like. Harry was an idiot to choose such a tale. An irritated annoyance stirred in her, close upon dislike. 'Anyhow, it's better than horrors,' she said hurriedly.

'Well,' put in her husband, letting forth a minor gust of laughter, 'it's possible, at any rate. Though one's as crazy as the other.' His meaning, was not wholly clear. 'If a man really loved,' he added in his blunt fashion, 'and was tricked by her, I could almost conceive his—'

'Oh, don't preach, John, for Heaven's sake. You're so dull in the pulpit.' But the interruption only served to emphasize the sentence which, otherwise, might have been passed over.

'Could conceive his finding life so worthless,' persisted the other, 'that—' He hesitated. 'But there, now, I promised I wouldn't,' he went on, laughing good-humouredly. Then, suddenly, as though in spite of himself, driven it seemed: 'Still, under such conditions he might show his contempt for human nature and for life by—'

It was a tiny stifled scream that stopped him this time.

'John, I hate, I loathe you, when you talk like that. And you've broken your word again.' She was more than petulant; a nervous anger sounded in her voice. It was the way he had said it, looking from them towards the window, that made her quiver. She felt him suddenly as a man; she felt afraid of him.

Her husband made no reply; he rose and looked at his watch leaning sideways towards the lamp, so that the expression of his face was shaded. 'Two o'clock,' he remarked. 'I think I'll take a turn through the house. I may find a workman asleep or something. Anyhow the light will soon come now.' He laughed; the expression of his face, his tone of voice, relieved her momentarily. He went out. They heard his heavy tread echoing down the carpetless long corridor.

Mortimer began at once. 'Did he mean anything?' he asked breathlessly. 'He doesn't love you the least little bit, anyhow. He never did. I do. You're wasted on him. You belong to me.' The words poured out. He covered her face with kisses. 'Oh, I didn't mean *that*,' he caught between the kisses.

The sailor released her, staring. 'What then?' he whispered. 'Do you think he saw us on the lawn?' he paused a moment, as she made no reply. The steps were audible in the distance still. 'I know!' he exclaimed suddenly. 'It's the blessed house he feels. That's what it is. He doesn't like it.'

A wind sighed through the room, making the papers flutter; something rattled; and Mrs Burley started. A loose end of rope swinging from the paperhanger's ladder caught her eye. She shivered slightly.

'He's different,' she replied in a low voice, nestling very close again, 'and so restless. Didn't you notice what he said just now—that under certain conditions he could understand a man'—she hesitated—'doing it,' she concluded, a sudden drop in her voice. 'Harry,' she looked full into his eyes, 'that's not like him. He didn't say that for nothing.'

'Nonsense! He's bored to tears, that's all. And the house is getting on your nerves, too.' He kissed her tenderly. Then, as she responded, he drew her nearer still and held her passionately, mumbling incoherent words, among which 'nothing to be afraid of' was distinguishable. Meanwhile, the steps were coming nearer. She pushed him away. 'You must behave yourself. I insist. You shall, Harry.' Then buried herself in his arms, her face hidden against his neck—only to disentangle herself the next instant and stand clear of him. 'I hate you, Harry,' she exclaimed sharply, a look of angry annoyance flashing across her face. 'And I *hate* myself. Why do you treat me—?' She broke off as the steps came closer, patted her hair straight, and stalked over to the open window.

'I believe after all you're only playing with me,' he said viciously. He stared in surprised disappointment, watching her. 'It's him you really love,' he added jealously. He looked and spoke like a petulant spoilt boy.

She did not turn her head. 'He's always been fair to me, kind and generous. He never blames me for anything. Give me a cigarette, and don't play the stage hero. My nerves are on edge, to tell you the truth.' Her voice jarred harshly, and as he lit her cigarette he noticed that her lips were trembling; his own hand trembled too. He was still holding the match, standing beside her at the window sill, when the steps crossed the threshold and John Burley came into the room. He went straight up to the table and turned the lamp down. 'It was smoking,' he remarked. 'Didn't you see?'

'I'm sorry, sir.' And Mortimer sprang forward too late to help him. 'It was the draught as you pushed the door open.' The big man said, 'Ah!' and drew a chair over, facing them. 'It's just the very house,' he told them. 'I've been through every room on this floor. It will make a splendid home, with very little alteration, too.' He turned round in his creaking wicker chair and looked up at his wife, who sat swinging her legs and smoking in the window embrasure. 'Lives will be saved inside these old walls. It's a good investment,' he went on, talking rather to himself it seemed. 'People will die here, too.'

'Hark!' Mrs Burley interrupted him. 'That noise—What is it?' A faint thudding sound in the corridor or in the adjoining room was audible, making all three look round quickly, listening for a repetition, which did not come. The papers fluttered on the table, the lamps smoked an instant.

'Wind,' observed Burley calmly, 'our little friend, the South Wind. Something blown over again, that's all.' But, curiously, the three of them stood up. 'I'll go and see,' he continued. 'Doors and windows are all open to let the paint dry.' Yet he did not move; he stood there watching a white moth that dashed round and round the lamp, flopping heavily now and again upon the bare deal table.

'Let me go, sir,' put in Mortimer eagerly. He was glad of the chance; for the first time he, too, felt uncomfortable. But there was another, who, apparently, suffered a discomfort greater than his own and was accordingly even more glad to get away.

'I'll go,' Mrs Burley announced, with decision. 'I'd like to. I haven't been out of this room since we came. I'm not an atom afraid.'

It was strange that for a moment she did not make a move either; it seemed as if she waited for something. For perhaps fifteen seconds no one stirred or spoke. She knew by the look in her lover's eyes that he had now become aware of the slight, indefinite change in her husband's manner, and was alarmed by it. The fear in him woke her contempt; she suddenly despised the youth, and was conscious of a new, strange yearning towards her husband; against her worked nameless pressure, troubling her being. There was an alteration in the room, she thought; something had come in. The trio stood listening to the gentle wind outside, waiting for the sound to be repeated; two careless, passionate young lovers and a man stood waiting, listening, watching in that room; yet it seemed there were five persons altogether and not three, for two guilty consciences stood apart and separate from their owners. John Burley broke the silence.

'Yes, you go, Nancy. Nothing to be afraid of—there. It's only the wind.' He spoke as though he meant it.

Mortimer bit his lips. 'I'll come with you,' he said instantly. He was confused. 'Let's all three go. I don't think we ought to be separated.'

But Mrs Burley was already at the door. 'I insist,' she said, with a forced laugh. 'I'll call if I'm frightened,' while her husband, saying nothing, watched her from the table.

'Take this,' said the sailor, flashing his electric torch as he went over to her. 'Two are better than one.' He saw her figure exquisitely silhouetted against the black corridor beyond; it was clear she wanted to go; any nervousness in her was mastered by a stronger emotion still; she was glad to be out of their presence for a bit. He had hoped to snatch a word of explanation in the corridor, but her manner stopped him. Something else stopped him, too.

'First door on the left,' he called out, his voice echoing down the empty length. 'That's the room where the noise came from. Shout if you want us.'

He watched her moving away, the light held steadily in front of her, but she made no answer, and he turned back to see John Burley lighting his cigar at the lamp chimney, his face thrust forward as he did so. He stood a second, watching him, as the lips sucked hard at the cigar to make it draw; the strength of the features was emphasized to sternness. He had meant to stand by the door and listen for the least sound from the adjoining room, but now found his whole attention focussed on the face above the lamp. In that minute he realized that Burley had wished—had meant—his wife to go. In that minute he also forgot his love, his shameless, selfish little mistress, his worthless, caddish little self. For John Burley looked up. He straightened slowly, puffing hard and quickly to make sure his cigar was lit, and faced him. Mortimer moved forward into the room, self-conscious, embarrassed, cold.

'Of course, it was only the wind,' he said lightly, his one desire being to fill the interval while they were alone with commonplaces. He did not wish the other to speak. 'Dawn wind, probably.' He glanced at his wrist-watch. 'It's half-past two already and the sun gets up at a quarter to four. It's light by now, I expect. The shortest night is never quite dark.' He rambled on confusedly, for the other's steady, silent stare embarrassed him. A faint sound of Mrs Burley moving in the next room made him stop a moment. He turned instinctively to the door, eager for an excuse to go.

'That's nothing,' said Burley, speaking at last and in a firm quiet voice. 'Only my wife, glad to be alone—my young and pretty wife. She's all right. I know her better than you do. Come in and shut the door.'

Mortimer obeyed. He closed the door and came close to the table, facing the other, who at once continued.

'If I thought,' he said, in that quiet deep voice, 'that you two were serious'—he uttered his words very slowly, with emphasis, with intense severity—'do you know what I should do? I will tell you, Mortimer. I should like one of us two—you or myself—to remain in this house, dead.'

His teeth gripped his cigar tightly; his hands were clenched; he went on through a half-closed mouth. His eyes blazed steadily.

'I trust her so absolutely—understand me?—that my belief in women, in human beings, would go. And with it the desire to live. Understand me?'

Each word to the young careless fool was a blow in the face, yet it was the softest blow, the flash of a big deep heart, that hurt the most. A dozen answers—denial, explanation, confession, taking all guilt upon himself—crowded his mind, only to be dismissed. He stood motionless and silent, staring hard into the other's eyes. No word passed his lips; there was no time in any case. It was in this position that Mrs Burley, entering at that moment, found them. She saw her husband's face; the other man stood with his back to her. She came in with a little nervous laugh. 'A bell-rope swinging in the wind and hitting a sheet of metal before the fireplace,' she informed them. And all three laughed together then, though each laugh had a different sound. 'But I hate this house,' she added. 'I wish we had never come.'

'The moment there's light in the sky,' remarked her husband quietly, 'we can leave. That's the contract; let's see it through. Another half-hour will do it. Sit down, Nancy, and have a bit of something.' He got up and placed a chair for her. 'I think I'll take another look around.' He moved slowly to the door. 'I may go out on to the lawn a bit, and see what the sky is doing.'

It did not take half a minute to say the words, yet to Mortimer it seemed as though the voice would never end. His mind was confused and troubled. He loathed himself, he loathed the woman through whom he had got into this awkward mess.

The situation had suddenly become extremely painful; he had never imagined such a thing; the man he had thought blind had after all seen everything—known it all along, watched them, waited. And the woman, he was now certain, loved her husband; she had fooled him, Mortimer, all along, amusing herself.

'I'll come with you, sir. Do let me,' he said suddenly. Mrs Burley stood pale and uncertain between them. She looked scared. What has happened, she was clearly wondering.

'No, no, Harry'—he called him 'Harry' for the first time— 'I'll be back in five minutes at the most. My wife mustn't be alone either.' And he went out.

The young man waited till the footsteps sounded some distance down the corridor, then turned, but he did not move forward; for the first time he let pass unused what he called 'an opportunity'. His passion had left him; his love, as he once thought it, was gone. He looked at the pretty woman near him, wondering blankly what he had ever seen there to attract him so wildly. He wished to Heaven he was out of it all. He wished he were dead. John Burley's words suddenly appalled him.

One thing he saw plainly—she was frightened. This opened his lips.

'What's the matter?' he asked, and his hushed voice shirked the familiar Christian name. 'Did you see anything?' He nodded his head in the direction of the adjoining room. It was the sound of his own voice addressing her coldly that made him abruptly see himself as he really was, but it was her reply, honestly given, in a faint even voice, that told him she saw her own self too with similar clarity. God, he thought, how revealing a tone, a single word can be!

'I saw—nothing. Only I feel uneasy—dear.' That 'dear' was a call for help.

'Look here,' he cried, so loud that she held up a warning finger, 'I'm—I've been a damned fool, a cad! I'm most frightfully ashamed. I'll do *anything*—anything to get it right.' He felt cold, naked, his worthlessness laid bare; she felt, he knew, the same. Each revolted suddenly from the other. Yet, he knew not quite how or wherefore this great change had thus abruptly come about, especially on her side. He felt that a bigger, deeper emotion than he could understand was working on them, making mere physical relationships seem empty, trivial, cheap and vulgar. His cold increased in the face of this utter ignorance.

'Uneasy?' he repeated, perhaps hardly knowing exactly why he said it. 'Good Lord, but he can take care of himself—'

'Oh, *he* is a man,' she interrupted; 'yes.'

Steps were heard, firm, heavy steps, coming back along the corridor. It seemed to Mortimer that he had listened to this sound of steps all night, and would listen to them till he died. He crossed to the lamp and lit a cigarette, carefully this time, turning the wick down afterwards. Mrs Burley also rose, moving towards the door, away from him. They listened a moment to these firm and heavy steps, the tread of a man, John Burley. A man—and a philanderer—flashed across Mortimer's brain like fire, contrasting the two with fierce contempt for himself. The tread became less audible. There was distance in it. It had turned in somewhere.

'There!' she exclaimed in a hushed tone. 'He's gone in.'

'Nonsense! It passed us. He's going out on to the lawn.'

The pair listened breathlessly for a moment, when the sound of steps came distinctly from the adjoining room, walking across the boards, apparently towards the window.

'There!' she repeated. 'He did go in.'

Silence of perhaps a minute followed, in which they heard each other's breathing. 'I don't like being alone—in there,' Mrs Burley said in a thin faltering voice, and moved as though to go out. Her hand was already on the knob of the door, when Mortimer stopped her with a violent gesture.

'Don't! For God's sake, don't!' he cried, before she could turn it. He darted forward. As he laid a hand upon her arm, a thud was audible through the wall. It was a heavy sound, and this time there was no wind to cause it.

'It's only that loose swinging thing,' he whispered thickly, a dreadful confusion blotting out clear thought and speech.

'There was no loose swaying thing at all,' she said in a failing voice, then reeled and swayed against him. 'I invented that. There was nothing.' As he caught her staring helplessly, it seemed to him that a face with lifted lids rushed up at him. He saw two terrified eyes in a patch of ghastly white. Her whisper followed, as she sank into his arms. 'It's John, he's—'

At which instant, with terror at its climax, the sound of steps suddenly became audible once more—the firm and heavy tread of John Burley coming out again into the corridor. Such was their amazement and relief that they neither moved nor spoke. The steps drew nearer. The pair seemed petrified; Mortimer did not remove his arms, nor did Mrs Burley attempt to release herself. They stared at the door and waited. It was pushed wider the next second, and John Burley stood beside them. He was so close he almost touched them—there in each other's arms.

'Jack, dear!' cried his wife, with a searching tenderness that made her voice seem strange.

He gazed a second at each in turn. 'I'm going out on to the lawn for a moment,' he said quietly. There was no expression on his face; he did not smile, he did not frown; he showed no feeling, no emotion—just looked into their eyes, and then withdrew round the edge of the door before either could utter a word in answer. The door swung to behind him.

He was gone. 'He's going to the lawn. He said so.' It was Mortimer speaking, but his voice shook and stammered. Mrs Burley had released herself. She stood now by the table, silent, gazing with fixed eyes at nothing, her lips parted, her expression vacant. Again, she was aware of an alteration in the room: something had gone out... He watched her a second, uncertain what to say or do. It was the face of a drowned person, occurred to him. Something intangible, yet almost visible stood between them in that narrow space. Something had ended, there before his eyes, definitely ended. The barrier between them rose higher, denser. Through this barrier her words came to him with an odd whispering remoteness.

'Harry. You saw? You noticed?'

'What d'you mean?' he said gruffly. He tried to feel angry, contemptuous, but his breath caught absurdly.

'Harry—he was different. The eyes, the hair, the'—her face grew like death—'the twist in his face—'

'What on earth are you saying? Pull yourself together.' He saw that she was trembling down the whole length of her body, as she leaned against the table for support. His own legs shook. He stared hard at her.

'Altered, Harry altered.' Her horrified whisper came at him like a knife. For it was true. He, too, had noticed something about the husband's appearance that was not quite normal. Yet, even while they talked, they heard him going down the carpetless stairs; the sounds ceased as he crossed the hall; then came the noise of the front door banging, the reverberation even shaking the room a little where they stood.

Mortimer went over to her side. He walked unevenly.

'My dear! For God's sake—this is sheer nonsense. Don't let yourself go like this. I'll put it straight with him—it's all my fault.' He saw by her face that she did not understand his words; he was saying the wrong thing altogether; her mind was utterly elsewhere. 'He's all right,' he went on hurriedly. 'He's not on the lawn now.'

He broke off at the sight of her. The horror that fastened on her brain plastered her face with deathly whiteness.

'That was not John at all,' she cried, a wail of misery and terror in her voice. She rushed to the window and he followed. To his immense relief a figure moving below was plainly visible. It was John Burley. They saw him in the faint grey of the dawn, as he crossed the lawn, going away from the house. He disappeared.

'There you are! See?' whispered Mortimer reassuringly. 'He'll be back in—' when a sound in the adjoining room, heavier, louder than before, cut appallingly across his words, and Mrs Burley, with that wailing scream, fell back into his arms. He caught her only just in time, for he stiffened into ice, daft with the uncomprehended terror of it all, and helpless as a child.

'Darling, my darling—oh, God!' He bent, kissing her face wildly. He was utterly distraught.

'Harry! John—oh, oh!' she wailed in her anguish. 'It took on his likeness. It deceived us to give him time. He's done it.'

She sat up suddenly. 'Go,' she said, pointing to the room beyond, then sank, fainting, a dead weight in his arms.

He carried her unconscious body to a chair, then entering the adjoining room he flashed his torch upon the body of her husband hanging from a bracket in the wall. He cut it down five minutes too late.

THE DEAD MAN OF VARLEY GRANGE

A Victorian Ghost Story by Anonymous

'Hallo, Jack! Where are you off to? Going down to the governor's place for Christmas?'

Jack Darent, who was in my old regiment, stood drawing on his dogskin gloves upon 23 December the year before last. He was equipped in a long Ulster and top hat, and a hansom, already loaded with a gun-case and portmanteau, stood awaiting him. He had a tall, strong figure, a fair, fresh-looking face, and the merriest blue eyes in the world. He held a cigarette between his lips, and late as was the season of the year there was a flower in his buttonhole. When did I ever see handsome Jack Darent and he did not look well dressed and well fed and jaunty? As I ran up the steps of the club he turned round and laughed merrily.

'My dear fellow, do I look the sort of man to be victimized at a family Christmas meeting? Do you know the kind of business they have at home? Three maiden aunts and a bachelor uncle, my eldest brother and his insipid wife, and all my sister's six noisy children at dinner. Church twice a day, and snapdragon between the services! No, thank you! I have a great affection for my old patents, but you don't catch me going in for that sort of national festival!'

'You irreverent ruffian!' I replied, laughing. 'Ah, if you were a married man—'

'Ah, if I were a married man!' replied Captain Darent with something that was almost a sigh, and then, lowering his voice, he said hurriedly, 'How is Miss Lester, Fred?'

'My sister is quite well, thank you,' I answered with becoming gravity; and it was not without spice of malice that I added, 'She has been going out to a great many halls and enjoying herself very much.'

Captain Darent looked profoundly miserable.

'I don't see how a poor fellow in a marching regiment, a younger son too, with nothing in the future to look to, is ever to marry nowadays,' he said almost savagely. 'When girls, too, are used to so much luxury and extravagance that they can't live without it. Matrimony is at a deadlock in this century, Fred, chiefly owing to the price of butchers' meat and bonnets. In fifty years' time it will become extinct and the country be depopulated. But I must be off, old man, or I shall miss my train.'

'You have never told me where you are going to, Jack.'

'Oh, I am going to stay with old Henderson in Westernshire; he has taken a furnished house with some first-rate pheasant shooting for a year. There are seven of us going—all bachelors, and all kindred spirits. We shall shoot all day and smoke half the night. Think what you have lost, old fellow, by becoming a Benedick!'

'In Westernshire, is it?' I inquired. 'Whereabouts is this place, and what is the name of it? For I am a Westernshire man by birth myself, and I know every place in the county.'

'Oh, it's a tumbledown sort of old house, I believe,' answered Jack carelessly. 'Gables and twisted chimneys outside, and uncomfortable spindle-legged furniture inside—you know the sort of thing; but the shooting is capital, Henderson says, and we must put up with our quarters. He has taken his French cook down, and plenty of liquor, so I've no doubt we shan't starve.'

'Well, but what is the name of it?' I persisted, with a growing interest in the subject.

'Let me see,' referring to a letter he pulled out of his pocket. 'Oh, here it is—Varley Grange.'

'Varley Grange!' I repeated, aghast. 'Why, it has not been inhabited for years.'

'I believe not,' answered Jack unconcernedly. 'The shooting has been let separately; but Henderson took a fancy to the house too and thought it would do for him, furniture and all, just as it is. My dear Fred, what are you looking so solemnly at me for?'

'Jack, let me entreat of you not to go to this place,' I said, laying my hand on his arm.

'Not go! Why, Lester, you must be mad! Why on earth shouldn't I go there?'

'There are stories—uncomfortable things said of that house.' I had not the moral courage to say, 'It is haunted,' and I felt myself how weak and childish was my attempt to deter him from his intended visit; only—I knew all about Varley Grange.

I think handsome Jack Darent thought privately that I was slightly out of my senses, for I am sure I looked unaccountably upset and dismayed by the mention of the name of the house that Mr Henderson had taken.

'I daresay it's cold and draughty and infested with rats and mice,' he said laughingly; 'and I have no doubt the creature-comforts will not be equal to Queen's Gate; but I stand pledged to go now, and I must be off this very minute, so have no time, old fellow, to inquire into the meaning of your sensational warning. Goodbye, and—and remember me to the ladies.'

He ran down the steps and jumped into the hansom.

'Write to me if you have time!' I cried out after him; but I don't think he heard me in the rattle of the departing cab. He nodded and smiled at me and was swiftly whirled out of sight.

As for me, I walked slowly back to my comfortable house in Queen's Gate. There was my wife presiding at the little five o'clock tea-table, our two fat, pink and white little children tumbling about upon the hearthrug amongst dolls and bricks, and two utterly spoilt and overfed pugs; and my sister Bella—who, between ourselves, was the prettiest as well as dearest girl in all London—sitting on the floor in her handsome brown velvet gown, resigning herself gracefully to be trampled upon by the dogs, and to have her hair pulled by the babies.

'Why, Fred, you look as if you had heard bad news,' said my wife, looking up anxiously as I entered.

'I don't know that I have heard of anything very bad; I have just seen Jack Darent off for Christmas,' I said, turning instinctively towards my sister. He was a poor man and a younger son, and of course a very bad match for the beautiful Miss Lester; but for all that I had an inkling that Bella was not quite indifferent to her brother's friend.

'Oh!' says that hypocrite. 'Shall I give you a cup of tea, Fred?'

It is wonderful how women can control their faces and pretend not to care a straw when they hear the name of their lover mentioned. I think Bella overdid it, she looked so supremely indifferent.

'Where on earth do you suppose he is going to stay, Bella?'

'Who? Oh, Captain Darent! How should I possibly know where he is going? Archie, pet, please don't poke the doll's head quite down Ponto's throat; I know he will bite it off if you do.'

This last observation was addressed to my son and heir.

'Well, I think you will be surprised when you hear: he is

going to Westernshire, to stay at Varley Grange.'

'*What!*' No doubt about her interest in the subject now! Miss Lester turned as white as her collar and sprang to her feet impetuously, scattering dogs, babies and toys in all directions away from her skirts as she rose.

'You cannot mean it, Fred! Varley Grange, why, it has not been inhabited for ten years; and the last time—Oh, do you remember those poor people who took it? What a terrible story it has!' She shuddered.

'Well, it is taken now,' I said, 'by a man I know, called Henderson—a bachelor; he has asked down a party of men for a week's shooting, and Jack Darent is one of them.'

'For Heaven's sake prevent him from going!' cried Bella, clasping her hands.

'My dear, he is gone!'

'Oh, then write to him—telegraph—tell him to come back!' she urged breathlessly.

'I am afraid it is no use,' I said gravely. 'He would not come back; he would not believe me; he would think I was mad.'

'Did you tell him anything?' she asked faintly.

'No, I had no time. I did say a word or two, but he began to laugh.'

'Yes, that is how it always is!' she said distractedly. 'People laugh and pooh-pooh the whole thing, and then they go there and see for themselves, and it is too late!'

She was so thoroughly upset that she left the room. My wife turned to me in astonishment; not being a Westernshire woman, she was not well up in the traditions of that venerable county.

'What on earth does it all mean, Fred?' she asked me in amazement. 'What is the matter with Bella, and why is she so distressed that Captain Darent is going to stay at that particular house?'

'It is said to be haunted, and—'

'You don't mean to say you believe in such rubbish, Fred?' interrupted my wife sternly, with a side-glance of apprehension at our first-born who, needless to say, stood by, all eyes and ears, drinking in every word of the conversation of his elders.

'I never know what I believe or what I don't believe,' I answered gravely. 'All I can say is that there are very singular traditions about that house, and that a great many credible witnesses have seen a very strange thing there, and that a great many disasters have happened to the persons who have seen it.'

'What has been seen, Fred? Pray tell me the story! Wait, I think I will send the children away.'

My wife rang the bell for the nurse, and as soon as the little ones had been taken from the room she turned to me again.

'I don't believe in ghosts or any such rubbish one bit, but I should like to hear your story.'

'The story is vague enough,' I answered.

'In the old days Varley Grange belonged to the ancient family of Varley, now completely extinct. There was, some hundred years ago, a daughter, famed for her beauty and her fascination. She wanted to marry a poor, penniless squire, who loved her devotedly. Her brother, Dennis Varley, the new owner of Varley Grange, refused his consent and shut his sister up in the nunnery that used to stand outside his park gates—there are a few ruins of it left still. The poor nun broke her vows and ran away in the night with her lover. But her brother pursued her and brought her back with him. The lover escaped, but the lord of Varley murdered his sister under his own roof, swearing that no scion of his race should live to disgrace and dishonour his ancient name.

'Ever since that day Dennis Varley's spirit cannot rest in its grave—he wanders about the old house at night time and those who have seen him are numberless. Now and then the pale, shadowy form of a nun flits across the old hall, or along the gloomy passages, and when both strange shapes are seen thus together misfortune and illness, and even death, is sure to pursue the luckless man who has seen them, with remorseless cruelty.'

'I wonder you believe in such rubbish,' says my wife at the conclusion of my tale.

I shrug my shoulders and answer nothing, for who are so obstinate as those who persist in disbelieving everything that they cannot understand?

◆

It was little more than a week later that, walking by myself along Pall Mall one afternoon, I suddenly came upon Jack Darent walking towards me.

'Hallo, Jack! Back again? Why, man, how odd you look!'

There was a change in the man that I was instantly aware of. His frank, careless face looked clouded and anxious, and the merry smile was missing from his handsome countenance.

'Come into the Club, Fred,' he said, taking me by the arm. 'I have something to say to you.'

He drew me into a corner of the Club's smoking-room.

'You were quite right. I wish to Heaven I had never gone to that house.'

'You mean—have you seen anything?' I inquired eagerly.

'I have seen *everything*,' he answered with a shudder. 'They say one dies within a year—'

'My dear fellow, don't be so upset about it,' I interrupted; I was quite distressed to see how thoroughly the man had altered.

'Let me tell you about it, Fred.'

He drew his chair close to mine and told me his story,

pretty nearly in the following words:

'You remember the day I went down you had kept me talking at the Club door; I had a race to catch the train; however, I just did it. I found the other fellows all waiting for me. There was Charlie Wells, the two Harfords, Colonel Riddell, who is such a crack shot, two fellows in the Guards, both pretty fair, a man called Thompson, a barrister, Henderson and myself— eight of us in all. We had a remarkably lively journey down, as you may imagine, and reached Varley Grange in the highest possible spirits. We all slept like tops that night.

'The next day we were out from eleven till dusk among the coverts, and a better day's shooting I never enjoyed in the whole course of my life, the birds literally swarmed. We bagged a hundred and thirty brace. We were all pretty well tired when we got home, and did full justice to a very good dinner and first-class Perrier-Jouet. After dinner we adjourned to the hall to smoke. This hall is quite the feature of the house. It is large and bright, panelled halfway up with sombre old oak, and vaulted with heavy carved oaken rafters. At the farther end runs a gallery, into which opened the door of my bedroom, and shut off from the rest of the passages by a swing door at either end.

'Well, all we fellows sat up there smoking and drinking brandy and soda, and jawing, you know—as men always do when they are together—about sport of all kinds, hunting and shooting and salmon-fishing; and I assure you not one of us had a thought in our heads beyond relating some wonderful incident of a long shot or big fence by which he would each cap the last speaker's experiences. We were just, I recollect, listening to a long story of the old Colonel's, about his experiences among bisons in Cachemire, when suddenly one of us—I can't remember who it was—gave a sort of shout and started to his feet, pointing up to the gallery behind us. We all turned round, and there—I give you my word of honour, Lester—stood a man leaning over the rail of the gallery, staring down upon us.

'We all saw him. Every one of us. Eight of us, remember. He stood there full ten seconds, looking down with horrible glittering eyes at us. He had a long tawny beard, and his hands, that were crossed together before him, were nothing but skin and bone. But it was his face that was so unspeakably dreadful. It was livid—the face of a dead man!'

'How was he dressed?'

'I could not see; he wore some kind of a black cloak over his shoulders, I think, but the lower part of his figure was hidden behind the railings. Well, we all stood perfectly speechless for, as I said, about ten seconds; and then the figure moved, backing slowly into the door of the room behind him, which stood open. It was the door of my bedroom! As soon as he had disappeared our senses seemed to return to us. There was a general rush for the staircase, and, as you may imagine, there was not a corner of the house that was left unsearched; my bedroom especially was ransacked in every part of it. But all in vain; there was not the slightest trace to be found of any living being. You may suppose that not one of us slept that night. We lighted every candle and lamp we could lay hands upon and sat up till daylight, but nothing more was seen.

'The next morning, at breakfast, Henderson, who seemed very much annoyed by the whole thing, begged us not to speak of it any more. He said that he had been told, before he had taken the house, that it was supposed to be haunted; but, not being a believer in such childish follies, he had paid but little attention to the rumour. He did not, however, want it talked about, because of the servants, who would be so easily frightened. He was quite certain, he said, that the figure we had seen last night must be somebody dressed up to practise a trick upon us, and he recommended us all to bring our guns down loaded after dinner, but meanwhile to forget the startling apparition as far as we could.

'We, of course, readily agreed to do as he wished, although I do not think that one of us imagined for a moment that any amount of dressing-up would be able to simulate the awful countenance that we had all of us seen too plainly. It would have taken a Hare or an Arthur Cecil, with all the theatrical appliances known only to those two talented actors, to have 'made-up' the face, that was literally that of a corpse. Such a person could not be amongst us—actually in the house—without our knowledge.

'We had another good day's shooting, and by degrees the fresh air and exercise and the excitement of the sport obliterated the impression of what we had seen in some measure from the minds of most of us. That evening we all appeared in the hall after dinner with our loaded guns besides us; but, although we sat up till the small hours and looked frequently up at the gallery at the end of the hall, nothing at all disturbed us that night.

'Two nights thus went by and nothing further was seen of the gentleman with the tawny beard. What with the good company, the good cheer and the pheasants, we had pretty well forgotten all about him.

'We were sitting as usual upon the third night, with our pipes and our cigars; a pleasant glow from the bright wood fire in the great chimney lighted up the old hall, and shed a genial warmth about us; when suddenly it seemed to me as if there came a breath of cold, chill air behind me, such as one feels when going down into some damp, cold vault or cellar.

'A strong shiver shook me from head to foot. Before even I saw it I *knew* that it was there.

'It leant over the railing of the gallery and looked down at us all just as it had done before. There was no change in the attitude, no alteration in the fixed, malignant glare in those stony, lifeless eyes; no movement in the white and bloodless features. Below, amongst the eight of us gathered there, there arose a panic of terror. Eight strong, healthy, well-educated nineteenth-century Englishmen, and yet I am not ashamed to say that we were paralysed with fear. Then one, more quickly recovering his senses than the rest, caught at his gun, that leant against the wide chimney-corner, and fired.

'The hall was filled with smoke, but as it cleared away every one of us could see the figure of our supernatural visitant slowly backing, as he had done on the previous occasion, into the chamber behind him, with something like a sardonic smile of scornful derision upon his horrible, death-like face.

'The next morning it is a singular and remarkable fact that four out of the eight of us received by the morning post—so they stated—letters of importance which called them up to town by the very first train! One man's mother was ill, another had to consult his lawyer, whilst pressing engagements, to which they could assign no definite name, called away the other two.

'There were left in the house that day but four of us— Wells, Bob Harford, our host, and myself. A sort of dogged determination not to be worsted by a scare of this kind kept us still there. The morning light brought a return of common sense and of natural courage to us. We could manage to laugh over last night's terrors whilst discussing our bacon and kidneys and hot coffee over the late breakfast in the pleasant morning-room, with the sunshine streaming cheerily in through the diamond-paned windows.

'It *must* be a delusion of our brains,' said one.

'Our host's champagne,' suggested another.

'A well-organized hoax,' opined a third.

'I will tell you what we will do,' said our host. 'Now that those other fellows have all gone—and I suppose we don't any of us believe much in those elaborate family reasons which have so unaccountably summoned them away—we four will sit up regularly night after night and watch for this thing, whatever it may be. I do not believe in ghosts. However, this morning I have taken the trouble to go out before breakfast to the Rector of the parish, an old gentleman who is well up in all the traditions of the neighbourhood, and I have learnt from him the whole of the supposed story of our friend of the tawny beard, which, if you like, I will relate to you.'

'Henderson then proceeded to tell us the tradition concerning the Dennis Varley who murdered his sister, the nun—a story which I will not repeat to you, Lester, as I see you know it already.

'The clergyman had furthermore told him that the figure of the murdered nun was also sometimes seen in the same gallery, but that this as a very rare occurrence. When both murderer and his victim are seen together terrible misfortunes are sure to assail the unfortunate living man who sees them; and if the nun's face is revealed death within the year is the doom of the ill-fated person who has seen it.

'"Of course," concluded our host, "I consider all these stories to be absolutely childish. At the same time I cannot help thinking that some human agency—probably a gang of thieves or housebreakers—is at work, and that we shall probably be able to unearth an organized system of villainy by which the rogues, presuming on the credulity of the persons who have inhabited the place, have been able to plant themselves securely among some secret passages and hidden rooms in the house, and have carried on their depredations undiscovered and unsuspected. Now, will all of you help me to unravel this mystery?"

'We all promised readily to do so. It is astonishing how brave we felt at eleven o'clock in the morning; what an amount of pluck and courage each man professed himself to be endued with; how lightly we jested about the 'old boy with the beard,' and what jokes we cracked about the murdered nun!

"'She would show her face oftener if she was good-looking. No fear of her looking at Bob Harford, he was too ugly. It was Jack Darent who was the showman of the party; she'd be sure to make straight for him if she could, he was always run after by the women," and so on, till we were all laughing loudly and heartily over our own witticisms. That was eleven o'clock in the morning.

'At eleven o'clock at night we could have given a very different report of ourselves.

'At eleven o'clock at night each man took up his appointed post in solemn and somewhat depressed silence.

'The plan of our campaign had been carefully organized by our host. Each man was posted separately with about thirty yards between them, so that no optical delusion, such as an effect of firelight upon the oak panelling, nor any reflection from the circular mirror over the chimney-piece, should be able to deceive more than one of us. Our host fixed himself in the very centre of the hall, facing the gallery at the end; Wells took up his position halfway up the short, straight flight of steps; Harford was at the top of the stairs upon the gallery itself; I was opposite to him at the further end. In this manner, whenever the figure—ghost or burglar—should appear, it must necessarily be between two of us, and be seen from both the right and the left side. We were prepared to believe that one amongst us might be deceived by his senses or by his imagination, but it was clear that two persons could not see the same object from a different point of view and be simultaneously deluded by any effect of light or any optical hallucination.

'Each man was provided with a loaded revolver, a brandy and soda and a sufficient stock of pipes or cigars to last him through the night. We took up our position at eleven o'clock exactly, and waited.

'At first we were all four very silent and, as I have said before, slightly depressed; but as the hour wore away and nothing was seen or heard we began to talk to each other. Talking, however, was rather a difficulty. To begin with, we had to shout—at least we in the gallery had to shout to Henderson, down in the hall; and though Harford and Wells could converse quite comfortably, I, not being able to see the latter at all from my end of the gallery; had to pass my remarks to him second-hand through Harford, who amused himself in misstating every intelligent remark that I entrusted him with; added to which natural impediments to the "flow of the soul," the elements thought fit to create such a hullabaloo without that conversation was rendered still further work of difficulty.

'I never remember such a night in all my life. The rain came down in torrents; the wind howled and shrieked wildly amongst the tall chimneys and the bare elm trees without. Every now and then there was a lull, and then, again and again, a long sobbing moan came swirling round and round the house, for all the world like the cry of a human being in agony. It was a night to make one shudder, and thank Heaven for a roof over one's head.

'We all sat on at our separate posts hour after hour, listening to the wind and talking at intervals; but as the time wore on insensibly we became less and less talkative, and a sort of depression crept over us.

'At last we relapsed into a profound silence; then suddenly there came upon us all that chill blast of air, like a breath from a charnel-house, that we had experienced before, and almost simultaneously a hoarse cry broke from Henderson in the body of the hall below, and from Wells halfway up the stairs.

'Harford and I sprang to our feet, and we too saw it.

'The dead man was slowly coming up the stairs. He passed silently up with a sort of still, gliding motion, within a few inches of poor Wells, who shrank back, white with terror, against the wall. Henderson rushed wildly up the staircase in pursuit, whilst Harford and I, up on the gallery, fell instinctively back at his approach.

'He passed between us. We saw the glitter of his sightless eyes—the shrivelled skin upon his withered face—the mouth that tell away like the mouth of a corpse, beneath his tawny beard. We felt the cold death-like blast that came with him, and the sickening horror of his terrible presence. Ah! Can I ever forget it?'

With a strong shudder Jack Darent buried his face in his hands, and seemed too much overcome for some minutes to be able to proceed.

'My dear fellow, are you *sure*?' I said in an awestruck whisper. He lifted his head.

'Forgive me, Lester; the whole business has shaken my nerves so thoroughly that I have not yet been able to get over it. But I have not yet told you the worst.'

'Good heavens—is there worse?' I ejaculated.

He nodded.

'No sooner,' he continued, 'had this awful creature passed us that Harford clutched at my arm and pointed to the farther end of the gallery.

'"Look!" he cried hoarsely, the nun!

'There, coming towards us from the opposite direction, was the veiled figure of a nun.

'There were the long, flowing black and white garments—the gleam of the crucifix at her neck—the jangle of her rosary-beads from her waist; but her face was hidden.

'A sort of desperation seized me. With a violent effort over myself, I went towards this fresh apparition.'

'It *must* be a hoax,' I said to myself, and there was a half-formed intention in my mind of wrenching aside the flowing draperies and of seeing for myself who and what it was. I strode towards the figure, I stood within half a yard of it. The nun raised her head slowly—and, Lester—*I saw her face!*'

There was a moment's silence.

'What was it like, Jack?' I asked him presently.

He shook his head.

'That I can never tell to any living creature.'

'Was it so horrible?'

He nodded assent, shuddering.

'And what happened next?'

'I believe I fainted. At all events I remembered nothing further. They made me go to the vicarage the next day. I was so knocked over by it all—I was quite ill. I could not have stayed in the house. I stopped there all yesterday, and I got up to town this morning. I wish to Heaven I had taken your advice, old man, and had never gone to that horrible house.'

'I wish you had, Jack,' I answered fervently. 'Do you know that I shall die within the year?' he asked me presently.

I tried to pooh-pooh it.

'My dear fellow, don't take the thing so seriously as all that. Whatever may be the meaning of these horrible apparitions, there can be nothing but an old wife's fable in that saying. Why on earth should you die—you of all people, a great strong fellow with a constitution of iron? You don't look much like dying!'

'For all that I shall die. I cannot tell you why I am so

certain—but I know that it will be so,' he answered in a low voice. 'And some terrible misfortune will happen to Harford— the other two never saw her—it is he and I who are doomed.'

◆

A year has passed away. Last summer fashionable society rang for a week or more with the tale of poor Bob Harford's misfortune. The girl whom he was engaged to, and to whom he was devotedly attached—young, beautiful and wealthy—ran away on the eve of her wedding-day with a drinking, swindling villain who had been turned out of ever so many clubs and tabooed for ages by every respectable man in town, and who had nothing but a handsome face and a fascinating manner to recommend him, and who by dint of these had succeeded in gaining a complete ascendancy over the fickle heart of poor Bob's lovely fiancée. As to Harford, he sold out and went off to the backwoods of Canada, and has never been heard of since.

And what of Jack Darent? Poor, handsome Jack, with his tall figure and his bright, happy face, and the merry blue eyes that had wiled Bella Lester's heart away! Alas! Far away in Southern Africa, poor Jack Darent lies in an unknown grave—slain by a Zulu assegai on the fatal plain of Isandula! And Bella goes about clad in sable garments, heavy-eyed and stricken with sore grief. A widow in heart, if not in name.

THE STORY OF THE SPANIARDS, HAMMERSMITH

E. and H. Heron

Lieutenant Roderick Houston, of H.M.S. *Sphinx*, had practically nothing beyond his pay, and he was beginning to be very tired of the West African station, when he received the pleasant intelligence that a relative had left him a legacy. This consisted of a satisfactory sum in ready money and a house in Hammersmith, which was rated at over £200 a year, and was said in addition to be comfortably furnished. Houston, therefore, counted on its rental to bring his income up to a fairly desirable figure. Further information from home, however, showed him that he had been rather premature in his expectations, whereupon, being a man of action, he applied for two months' leave, and came home to look after his affairs himself.

When he had been a week in London, he arrived at the conclusion that he could not possibly hope, single-handed, to tackle the difficulties which presented themselves. He accordingly wrote the following letter to his friend, Flaxman Low:

The Spaniards, Hammersmith, 23-3-1892

Dear Low,—Since we parted some three years ago, I have heard very little of you. It was only yesterday that I met our mutual friend, Sammy Smith ('Silkworm' of our schooldays), who told me that your studies have developed in a new direction, and that you are now a good deal interested in psychical subjects. If this be so, I hope to induce you to come and stay with me here for a few days by promising to introduce you to a problem in your own line. I am just now living at 'The Spaniards', a house that has lately been left to me, and which in the first instance was built by an old fellow named Van Nuysen, who married a great-aunt of mine. It is a good house, but there is said to be 'something wrong' with it. It lets easily, but unluckily the tenants cannot be persuaded to remain above a week or two. They complain that the place is haunted by something—presumably a ghost—because its vagaries bear just that brand of inconsequence which stamps the common run of manifestations.

It occurs to me that you may care to investigate the matter with me. If so, send me a wire when to expect you.

Yours ever,
Roderick Houston

Houston waited in some anxiety for an answer. Low was the sort of man one could rely on in almost any emergency. Sammy Smith had told him a characteristic anecdote of Low's career at Oxford, where, although his intellectual triumphs may be forgotten, he will always be remembered by the story that when Sands, of Queen's, fell ill on the day before the Varsity sports, a telegram was sent to Low's rooms: 'Sands ill. You must do the hammer for us.' Low's reply was pithy: 'I'll be there.' Thereupon he finished the treatise upon which he was engaged, and the next day his strong, lean figure was to be seen swinging the hammer amidst vociferous cheering, for that was the occasion on which he not only won the event, but beat the record.

On the fifth day Low's answer came from Vienna. As he read it, Houston recalled the high forehead, long neck—with its accompanying low collar—and thin moustache of his scholarly, athletic friend and smiled. There was so much more in Flaxman Low than anyone gave him credit for.

> My Dear Houston,—Very glad to hear of you again. In response to your kind invitation, I thank you for the opportunity of meeting the ghost, and still more for the pleasure of your companionship. I came here to inquire into a somewhat similar affair. I hope, however, to be able to leave tomorrow, and will be with you some time on Friday evening.
>
> Very sincerely yours,
Flaxman Low.
>
> P.S.—By the way, will it be convenient to give your servants a holiday during the term of my visit, as, if my investigations are to be of any value, not a grain of dust must be disturbed in your house, excepting by ourselves? —F.L.

'The Spaniards' was within some fifteen minutes' walk of Hammersmith Bridge. Set in the midst of a fairly respectable neighbourhood, it presented an odd contrast to the commonplace dullness of the narrow streets crowded about it. As Flaxman Low drove up in the evening light, he reflected that the house might have come from the back of beyond—it gave an impression of something old-world and something exotic.

It was surrounded by a ten-foot wall, above which the upper storey was visible, and Low decided that this intensely English house still gave some curious suggestion of the tropics. The interior of the house carried out the same idea, with its sense of space and air, cool tints and wide, matted passages.

'So you have seen something yourself since you came?' Low said, as they sat at dinner, for Houston had arranged that meals should be sent in for them from a hotel.

'I've heard tapping up and down the passage upstairs. It is an uncarpeted landing which runs the whole length of the house. One night, when I was quicker than usual, I saw what looked like a bladder disappear into one of the bedrooms—your room it is to be, by the way—and the door closed behind it,' replied Houston discontentedly. 'The usual meaningless antics of a ghost.'

'What had the tenants who lived here to say about it?' went on Low.

'Most of the people saw and heard just what I have told you, and promptly went away. The only one who stood out for a little while was old Filderg—you know the man? Twenty years ago he made an effort to cross the Australian deserts—he stopped for eight weeks. When he left he saw the house-agent, and said he was afraid he had done a little shooting practice in the upper passage, and he hoped it wouldn't count against him in the bill, as it was done in defence of his life. He said something had jumped on to the bed and tried to strangle him. He described it as cold and glutinous, and he pursued it down the passage, firing at it. He advised the owner to have the house pulled down; but, of course, my cousin did nothing of the kind. It's a very good house, and he did not see the sense of spoiling his property.'

'That's very true,' replied Flaxman Low, looking round. 'Mr Van Nuysen had been in the West Indies, and kept his liking for spacious rooms.'

'Where did you hear anything about him?' asked Houston in surprise.

'I have heard nothing beyond what you told me in your letter; but I see a couple of bottles of Gulf weed and a lace-plant ornament, such as people used to bring from the West Indies in former days.'

'Perhaps I should tell you the history of the old man,' said Houston doubtfully; 'but we aren't proud of it!'

Flaxman Low considered a moment.

'When was the ghost seen for the first time?'

'When the first tenant took the house. It was let after old Van Nuysen's time.'

'Then it may clear the way if you will tell me something of him.'

'He owned sugar plantations in Trinidad, where he passed the greater part of his life, while his wife mostly remained in England—incompatibility of temper it was said. When he came home for good, and built this house they still lived apart, my aunt declaring that nothing on earth would persuade her to return to him. In course of time he became a confirmed invalid, and then insisted on my aunt joining him. She lived here for perhaps a year, when she was found dead in bed one morning—in your room.'

'What caused her death?'

'She had been in the habit of taking narcotics, and it was supposed that she smothered herself while under their influence.'

'That doesn't sound very satisfactory,' remarked Flaxman Low. 'Her husband was satisfied with it anyhow, and it was no one else's business. The family were only too glad to have the affair hushed up.'

'And what became of Mr Van Nuysen?'

'That I can't tell you. He disappeared a short time after. Search was made for him in the usual way, but nobody knows to this day what became of him.'

'Ah, that was strange, as he was such an invalid,' said Low, and straightway fell into a long fit of abstraction, from which he was roused by hearing Houston curse the incurable foolishness and imbecility of ghostly behaviour. Flaxman woke up at this. He broke a walnut thoughtfully and began in a gentle voice: 'My dear fellow, we are apt to be hasty in our condemnation of the general behaviour of ghosts. It may appear incalculably foolish in our eyes, and I admit there often seems to be a total absense of any apparent object or intelligent action. But remember that what appears to us to be foolishness may be wisdom in the spirit world, since our unready senses can only catch broken glimpses of what is, I have not the slightest doubt, a coherent whole, if we could trace the connection.'

'There may be something in that,' replied Houston indifferently. 'People naturally say that this ghost is the ghost of old Van Nuysen. But what connection can possibly exist between what I have told you of him and the manifestations—a tapping up and down the passage and the drawing about of a bladder-like a child at play? It sounds idiotic!'

'Certainly. Yet, it need not necessarily be so. There are isolated facts, we must look for the links which lie between. Suppose a saddle and a horseshoe were to be shown to a man who had never seen a horse, I doubt whether he, however intelligent, could evolve the connecting idea! The ways of spirits are strange to us simply because we need further data to help us to interpret them.'

'It's a new point of view,' returned Houston, 'but upon my word, you know, Low, I think you're wasting your time!'

Flaxman Low smiled slowly; his grave, melancholy face brightened.

'I have,' said he, 'gone somewhat deeply into the subject. In other sciences one reasons by analogy. Psychology is unfortunately a science with a future but without a past, or more probably it is a lost science of the ancients. However that may be, we stand today on the frontier of an unknown world, and progress is the result of individual effort; each solution of difficult phenomena forms a step towards the solution of the next problem. In this case, for example, the bladder-like object may be the key to the mystery.'

Houston yawned.

'It all seems pretty senseless, but perhaps you may be able to read reason into it. If it were anything tangible, anything a man could meet with his fists, it would be easier.'

'I entirely agree with you. But suppose we deal with this affair as it stands, on similar lines, I mean on prosaic, rational lines, as we should deal with a purely human mystery.'

'My dear fellow,' returned Houston, pushing his chair back from the table wearily, 'you shall do just as you like, only get rid of the ghost!'

For some time after Low's arrival nothing very special happened. The tappings continued, and more than once Low had been in time to see the bladder disappear into the closing door of his bedroom, though, unluckily, he never chanced to be inside the room on these occasions, and however quickly he followed the bladder, he never succeeded in seeing anything further. He made a thorough examination of the house, and left no space unaccounted for in his careful measurement. There were no cellars, and the foundation of the house consisted of a thick layer of concrete.

At length, on the sixth night, an event took place, which, as

Flaxman Low remarked, came very near to putting an end to the investigations as far as he was concerned. For the preceding two nights, he and Houston had kept watch in the hope of getting a glimpse of the person or thing which tapped so persistently up and down the passage. But they were disappointed, for there were no manifestations. On the third evening, therefore, Low went off to his room a little earlier than usual, and fell asleep almost immediately.

He says he was awakened by feeling a heavy weight upon his feet, something that seemed inert and motionless. He recollected that he had left the gas burning, but the room was now in darkness.

Next, he was aware that the thing on the bed had slowly shifted, and was gradually travelling up towards his chest. How it came on the bed he had no idea. Had it leaped or climbed? The sensation he experienced as it moved was of some ponderous, pulpy body, not crawling or creeping, but spreading! It was horrible! He tried to move his lower limbs, but could not because of the deadening weight. A feeling of drowsiness began to overpower him, and a deadly cold, such as he said he had before felt at sea when in the neighbourhood of icebergs, chilled upon the air.

With a violent struggle he managed to free his arms, but the thing grew more irresistible as it spread upwards. Then he became conscious of a pair of glassy eyes, with livid, everted lids, looking into his own. Whether they were human eyes or beast eyes, he could not tell, but they were watery, like the eyes of a dead fish, and gleamed with a pale, internal lustre.

Then he owns he grew afraid. But he was still cool enough to notice one peculiarity about this ghastly visitant—although the head was within a few inches of his own, he could detect no breathing. It dawned upon him that he was about to be suffocated, for, by the same method of extension, the thing was now coming over his face! It felt cold and clammy, like a mass of mucilage or a monstrous snail. And every instant the weight became greater. He is a powerful man, and he struck with his fists again and again at the head. Some substance yielded under the blows with a sickening sensation of bruised flesh.

With a lucky twist he raised himself in the bed and battered away with all the force he was capable of in his cramped position. The only effect was an occasional shudder or quake that ran through the mass as his half-arm blows rained upon it. At last, by chance, his hand knocked against the candle beside him. In a moment he recollected the matches. He seized the box, and struck a light.

As he did so, the lump slid to the floor. He sprang out of bed, and lit the candle. He felt a cold touch upon his leg, but when he looked down there was nothing to be seen. The door, which he had locked overnight, was now open, and he rushed out into the passage. All was still and silent with the throbbing vacancy of night time.

After searching round, he returned to his room. The bed still gave ample proof of the struggle that had taken place, and by his watch he saw the hour to be between two and three.

As there seemed nothing more to be done, he put on his dressing-gown, lit his pipe, and sat down to write an account of the experience he had just passed through for the Psychical Research Society—from which paper the above is an abstract.

He is a man of strong nerves, but he could not disguise from himself that he had been at handgrips with some grotesque form of death. What might be the nature of his assailant he could not determine, but his experience was supported by the attack which had been made on Filderg, and also—it was impossible to avoid the conclusion—by the manner of Mrs Van Nuysen's death.

He thought the whole situation over carefully in connection with the tapping and the disappearing bladder, but, turn these events how he would, he could make nothing of them. They were entirely incongruous. A little later he went and made a shakedown in Houston's room.

'What was the thing!' asked Houston, when Low had ended his story of the encounter.

Low shrugged his shoulders.

'At least, it proves that Filderg did not dream,' he said.

'But this is monstrous! We are more in the dark than ever. There's nothing for it but to have the house pulled down. Let us leave today.'

'Don't be in a hurry, my dear fellow. You would rob me of a very great pleasure; besides, we may be on the verge of some valuable discovery. This series of manifestations is even more interesting than the Vienna mystery I was telling you of.'

'Discovery or not,' replied the other, 'I don't like it.'

The first thing next morning Low went out for a quarter of an hour. Before breakfast a man with a barrowful of sand came into the garden. Low looked up from his paper, leant out of the window, and gave some order.

When Houston came down a few minutes later he saw the yellowish heap on the lawn with some surprise.

'Hullo! What's this?' he asked.

'I ordered it,' replied Low.

'All right. What's it for?'

'To help us in our investigations. Our visitor is capable of being felt, and he or it left a very distinct impression on the bed. Hence I gather it can also leave an impression on sand. It would be an immense advance if we could arrive at any correct notion of what sort of feet the ghost walks on. I propose to spread a layer of this sand in the upper passage, and the result should be footmarks if the tapping comes tonight.'

That evening the two men made a fire in Houston's bedroom, and sat there smoking and talking, to leave the ghost 'a free run for once', as Houston phrased it. The tapping was heard at the usual hour, and presently the accustomed pause at the other end of the passage and the quiet closing of the door.

Low heaved a long sigh of satisfaction as he listened.

'That's my bedroom door,' he said: 'I know the sound of it perfectly. In the morning, and with the help of daylight, we shall see what we shall see.'

As soon as there was light enough for the purpose of examining the footprints, Low roused Houston.

Houston was as full of excitement as a boy, but his spirits fell by the time he had passed from end to end of the passage.

'There are marks,' he said, 'but they are as perplexing as everything else about this haunting brute, whatever it is. I suppose you think this is the print left by the thing which attacked you the night before last?'

'I fancy it is,' said Low, who was still bending over the floor eagerly. 'What do you make of it, Houston?'

'The brute has only one leg, to start with,' replied Houston, 'and that leaves the mark of a large, clawless pad! It's some animal—some ghoulish monster!'

'On the contrary,' said Low, 'I think we have now every reason to conclude that it is a man.'

'A man? What man ever left footmarks like these?'

'Look at these hollows and streaks at the sides; they are the traces of the sticks we have heard tapping.'

'You don't convince me,' returned Houston doggedly.

'Let us wait another twenty-four hours, and tomorrow night, if nothing further occurs, I will give you my conclusions. Think it over. The tapping, the bladder, and the fact that

Mr Van Nuysen had lived in Trinidad. Add to these things this single pad-like print. Does noting strike you by way of a solution?'

Houston shook his head.

'Nothing. And I fail to connect any of these things with what happened both to you and Filderg.'

'Ah! Now,' said Flaxman Low, his face clouding a little, 'I confess you lead me into a somewhat different region, though to me the connection is perfect.'

Houston raised his eyebrows and laughed.

'If you can unravel this tangle of hints and events and diagnose the ghost, I shall be extremely astonished,' he said. 'What can you make of the footless impression?'

'Something, I hope. In fact, that mark may be a clue—an outrageous one, perhaps, but still a clue.'

That evening the weather broke, and by night the storm had risen to a gale, accompanied by sharp bursts of rain.

'It's a noisy night,' remarked Houston; 'I don't suppose we'll hear the ghost, supposing it does turn up.'

This was after dinner, as they were about to go into the smoking-room. Houston, finding the gas low in the hall, stopped to turn it higher; at the same time asking Low to see if the jet on the upper landing was also alight.

Flaxman Low glanced up and uttered a slight exclamation, which brought Houston to his side.

Looking down at them from over the banisters was a face—a blotched, yellowish face, flanked by two swollen, protruding ears, the whole aspect being strangely leonine. It was but a glimpse, a clash of meeting glances, as it were a glare of defiance, and the face was quickly withdrawn as the two men literally leapt up the stairs.

'There's nothing here,' exclaimed Houston, after a search

had been carried out through every room above.

'I didn't suppose we'd find anything,' returned Low.

'This fairly knots up the thread,' said Houston. 'You can't pretend to unravel it now.'

'Come down,' said Low briefly; 'I'm ready to give you my opinion, such as it is.'

Once in the smoking-room, Houston busied himself in turning on all the light he could procure, then he saw to securing the windows, and piled up an immense fire, while Flaxman Low, who, as usual, had a cigarette in his mouth, sat on the edge of the table and watched him with some amusement.

'You saw that abominable face?' cried Houston, as he threw himself into a chair. 'It was as material as yours or mine. But where did he go to? He must be somewhere about.'

'We saw him clearly. That is sufficient for our purpose.'

'You are very good at enumerating points, Low. Now just listen to my list. The difficulties grow with every fresh discovery. We're at a deadlock now, I take it? The sticks and the tapping point to an old man, the playing with a bladder to a child; the footmark might be the pad of a tiger minus claws, yet the thing that attacked you at night was cold and pulpy. And, lastly, by way of a wind-up, we see a lion-like, human face! If you can make all these items square with each other, I'll be happy to hear what you have got to say.'

'You must first allow me to ask you a question. I understood you to say that no blood relationship existed between you and old Mr Van Nuysen?'

'Certainly not. He was quite an outsider,' answered Houston brusquely.

'In that case you are welcome to my conclusions. All the things you have mentioned point to one explanation. This house is haunted by the ghost of Mr Van Nuysen, and he was a leper.'

Houston stood up and stared at his companion.

'What a horrible notion! I must say I fail to see how you have arrived at such a conclusion.'

'Take the chain of evidence in a rather different order,' said Low. 'Why should a man tap with a stick?'

'Generally because he's blind.'

'In cases of blindness, one stick is used for guidance. Here we have two for support.'

'A man who has lost the use of his feet.'

'Exactly; a man who has from some cause partially lost the use of his feet.'

'But the bladder and the lion-like face?' went on Houston.

'The bladder, or what seemed to us to resemble a bladder, was one of his feet, contorted by the disease and probably swathed in linen, which foot he dragged rather than used; consequently, in passing through a door, for example, he would be in the habit of drawing it in after him. Now, as regards the single footmark we saw. In one form of leprosy, the smaller bones of the extremities frequently fall away. The pad-like impression was, as I believe, the mark of the other foot—a toeless foot which he used, because in a more advanced stage of the disease the maimed hand or foot heals and becomes callous.'

'Go on,' said Houston; 'it sounds as if it might be true. And the lion-like face I can account for myself. I have been in China, and have seen it before in lepers.'

'Mr Van Nuysen had been in Trinidad for many years, as we know, and while there he probably contracted the disease.'

'I suppose so. After his return,' added Houston, 'he shut himself up almost entirely, and gave out that he was a martyr to rheumatic gout, this awful thing being the true explanation.'

'It also accounts for Mrs Van Nuysen's determination not to return to her husband.'

Houston appeared much disturbed.

'We can't drop it here, Low,' he said, in a constrained voice. 'There is a good deal more to be cleared up yet. Can you tell me more?'

'From this point I find myself on less certain ground,' replied Low unwillingly. 'I merely offer a suggestion, remember—I don't ask you to accept it. I believe Mrs Van Nuysen was murdered!'

'What?' exclaimed Houston. 'By her husband?'

'Indications tend that way.'

'But, my good fellow—'

'He suffocated her and then made away with himself. It is a pity that his body was not recovered. The condition of the remains would be the only really satisfactory test of my theory. If the skeleton could even now be found, the fact that he was a leper would be finally settled.'

There was a prolonged pause until Houston put another question.

'Wait a minute, Low,' he said. 'Ghosts are admittedly immaterial. In this instance our spook has an extremely palpable body. Surely this is rather unusual? You have made everything else more or less plain. Can you tell me why this dead leper should have tried to murder you and old Filderg? And also how he came to have the actual physical power to do so?'

Low removed his cigarette to look thoughtfully at the end of it. 'Now I lapse into the purely theoretical,' he answered. 'Cases have been known where the assumption of diabolical agency is apparently justifiable.'

'Diabolical agency?—I don't follow you.'

'I will try to make myself clear, though the subject is still in a stage of vagueness and immaturity. Van Nuysen committed a murder of exceptional atrocity, and afterwards killed himself. Now, bodies of suicides are known to be peculiarly susceptible to spiritual influences, even to the point of arrested corruption. Add to this our knowledge that the highest aim of an evil spirit is to gain possession of a material body. If I carried out my theory to its logical conclusion, I should say that Van Nuysen's body is hidden somewhere on these premises—that this body is intermittently animated by some spirit, which at certain periods is forced to re-enact the gruesome tragedy of the Van Nuysens. Should any living person chance to occupy the position of the first victim, so much the worse for him!'

For some minutes Houston made no remark on this singular expression of opinion.

'But have you ever met with anything of the sort before?' he said at last.

'I can recall,' replied Flaxman Low thoughtfully, 'quite a number of cases which would seem to bear out this hypothesis. Among them a curious problem of haunting exhaustively examined by Busner in the early part of 1888, at which I was myself lucky enough to assist. Indeed, I may add that the affair which I have recently been engaged upon in Vienna offers some rather similar features. There, however, we had to stop short of excavation, by which alone any specific results might have been attained.'

'Then you are of the opinion,' said Houston, 'that pulling the house to pieces might cast some further light upon this affair?'

'I cannot see any better course,' said Mr Low.

Then Houston closed the discussion by a very definite declaration.

'This house shall come down!'

So 'The Spaniards' was pulled down.

The work of demolition, begun at the earliest possible moment, did not occupy very long, and during its early stages, under the boarding at an angle of the landing was found a skeleton. Several of the phalanges were missing, and other indications also established beyond doubt the fact that the remains were the remains of a leper.

The skeleton is now in the museum of one of our city hospitals. It bears a scientific ticket, and is the only evidence extant of the correctness of Mr Flaxman Low's methods and the possible truth of his extraordinary theories.

DEATH IN THE KITCHEN

Milward Kennedy

Rupert Morrison straightened himself, drawing a deep breath. He glanced round the little kitchen, deliberately looking at the figure which lay huddled on the floor; huddled, but yet in an attitude which Morrison hoped was as natural as its unnatural circumstances would permit. For the head was inside the oven of the rusty-looking gas-stove.

He wondered whether the cushion on which the head rested was a natural or an unnatural touch. He decided that if he were committing suicide, he would try to make even a gas-oven as comfortable as possible.

He walked silently (for he was in stockinged feet) into the passage, and so to the sitting-room. The curtains he had drawn so carefully that he had had no hesitation in leaving on the lights. Quickly but methodically he set to work. Nothing must be left which connected him in any way with George Manning. In any way? Well, how about that package addressed not to Manning but to himself from the local grocer? Probably it had been delivered in error. Still, he must take no chances. He put it aside for future attention.

Where did Manning keep his papers? He was a careless

devil, not likely to hide them securely or ingeniously. No, here they were in the writing-table. Only six that concerned Rupert Morrison; was that really all? He untied the packet and read each of the six. His cheeks reddened as he read; they were certainly damning. What a fool he had been in those days: still, he had been wise enough to remember it when Manning turned up out of the blue (he could not have spent all the interval in gaol?) and started his blackmail. George Manning on the other hand had grown foolish, for he had not troubled to discover whether his victim had changed.

Morrison's clumsy gloved hands thrust the packet into his breast pocket. He considered. He had plenty of time. Manning, he knew, lived alone in the cottage, and had few friends, certainly none who were likely to call on him; his domestic staff was limited to an old woman from the distant village who came in for part of the day.

The important thing was to be thorough. He had no alibi, and knew that it would be folly to fake one. Provided that there was nothing to show that he had a motive for wanting Manning dead, he would not have to account for his own whereabouts; his tale of a country tramp across the fields and through the woods would not even be wanted. Outside the cottage there was, he knew, nothing to suggest any relationship between Manning and himself save such as might exist between two men, friends long ago in schooldays, who had drifted apart, and then by chance met again: the one respected and prosperous, the other—George Manning.

At last he was satisfied with the sitting-room, but there were still the two bedrooms. Bare shabby rooms they were, and they did not keep him long. Down to the 'parlour' once more. He was reluctant to leave it, for there, if anywhere, he would leave behind a key to the truth.

But he could think of nothing more, except the tumblers on the table and the grocer's package.

There must be only one glass, of course; one must be washed and put away in the kitchen. The other? It, too, must be washed, for when it was found there must be no trace of anything more deadly in it than whisky. Of course, he could wash it and provide fresh prints of Manning's fingers.

He had to make two journeys to the kitchen with the 'properties' for the scene which he must set.

Soon one tumbler was back in the cupboard; the other, on which, after he had washed it, he had carefully pressed Manning's limp hand, stood on the table, a trace of neat whisky in it. Beside it the bottle, nearly empty; Manning certainly had been putting it away. That, no doubt, was why he had been so unnoticing when Morrison (none too neatly) had emptied his little flask into the tumbler. He gave a worried glance at the body; if the dose had been too strong the whole plan might go astray. But that was absurd—he had felt the pulse only a minute ago.

And now the last detail—to put that half-sheet of paper on the table. He placed it to look as if it had been folded to catch the eye; he dared not forge a superscription to the coroner.

He smiled; it was a bit of luck that those words so exactly filled a half-sheet in Manning's letter. Directly he had received it, months ago, he had seen its possible value.

'I am tired of it all. Who can blame me for taking the easiest way? So take it smiling—as I propose to do.—GEORGE MANNING.' But it was cash that Manning had meant to take with a smile—not coal-gas.

There. And the window tight shut. Now to turn on the gas, leave the electric light burning, and be gone. Footprints? No, his stockinged feet had left none, he was sure. Boots on. Quietly out by the back door, with nothing to carry but a walking stick and that grocer's packet...

Not a soul did Morrison meet on his way home, and when he had emptied the packet of sugar down the wash basin, and in the same way disposed of the ashes of its cover and of those six letters he took another deep breath—of relief this time... Naturally the police would come to him, for he was a man of standing and he was known to be on terms of acquaintance with Manning. He would be able to tell them that the 'poor chap' had seemed very neurotic... His 'Good morning' smile as the sergeant was shown in at these thoughts as well as a matter of policy.

'Yes, sergeant, I know him slightly.' By Jove! As nearly as no matter he had said 'knew'; he must watch his tongue.

'D'you recognize this, sir?'

Good God! What was the man holding up? A pocketbook, dark blue, with a monogram. He put his hand to his breast pocket. No—could he. He had an appalling memory of pushing those papers into his pocket. His gloved fingers had felt so clumsy. *Could* he have pulled it out and left it lying on the carpet—there?

He put out his hand; his power of speech seemed to have vanished. He took the pocketbook, half surprised that the sergeant allowed him to do so, and turned it over and over, and stared at it. What use was a denial?

The sergeant was speaking. Was he warning him that anything he might say...?

'That's the boy from Bayley's, the grocer, sir. Seems he delivered the wrong parcel—one for you, it was. Left it last evening at the cottage. Went first thing to get it back. Couldn't get a reply and the front door was locked, so he went round to the back. It seems the back door was open—of course, sir, he hadn't no right to go in, but...'

Why *would* the fool bother about that? Go on, man. My heart won't stand this.

'Electric light burning in the kitchen and this Manning lying with his head inside the oven. Gave the boy a shock, so he says, but if you ask me... Anyways, he came along on his bike to me—I found the pocketbook, sir, in the sitting-room. I thought I'd have a word with you. You see, this Mr Manning—well—sir, there's a police record.'

Why must he pause? Did he expect an answer? Morrison could only stare, his lips trembling.

'Course, sir. You may have given it to him. Or it may just have been an accident...'

What was 'it'? Even if he could have spoken, Morrison would have refused now.

'But apart from that, sir—his record and that, I mean—it struck me there was something queer about Manning. And I thought maybe you could help me. That gas-oven, sir, that looks like suicide, doesn't it, sir?'

'Yes—I suppose so.'

Was that really his voice?

'There was a bottle of whisky on the table—that came from Baylcy's yesterday afternoon, too, and it was empty all but a drain this morning. Maybe it was that that did it...'

What *had* gone wrong? How had this local bumpkin stumbled on the truth?

'At any rate, sir, whisky or lunacy, would you have thought anyone, drunk or sober, could put his head in a gas-oven and turn the tap—and forget the gas was cut off because he hadn't paid the bill? I can understand how it is; he's forgotten every blamed thing about what happened last night, but—Hallo, sir, what's up?'

Rupert Morrison was lying at the sergeant's feet.

HOICHI THE EARLESS

Lafcadio Hearn

More than seven hundred years ago, at Dan-no-ura, in the Straits of Shimonoséki, was fought the last battle of the long contest between the Heiké, or Taira clan, and the Genji, or Minamoto clan. There the Heiké perished utterly, with their women and children, and their infant emperor likewise—now remembered as Antoku Tenno. And that sea and shore have been haunted for seven hundred years... Elsewhere I told you about the strange crabs found there, called Heiké crabs, which have human faces on their backs, and are said to be the spirits of Heiké warriors. But there are many strange things to be seen and heard along that coast. On dark nights thousands of ghostly fires hover about the beach, or flit above the waves—pale lights which the fishermen call *Oni-bi,* or demon-fires; and, whenever the winds are up, a sound of great shouting comes from that sea, like a clamour of battle.

In former years the Heiké were much more restless than they are now. They would rise about ships passing in the night, and try to sink them; and at all times they would watch for swimmers, to pull them down. It was in order to appease those dead that the Buddhist temple, Amidaji, was built at Akamagaséki. A cemetery was also made close by, near the beach; and within it were set up monuments inscribed with the names of the drowned emperor and of his great vassals; and Buddhist services were regularly performed there, on behalf of the spirits. After the temple had been built, and the tombs erected, the Heiké gave less trouble than before; but they continued to do queer things at intervals—proving that they had not found perfect peace.

Some centuries ago, there lived at Akamaséki a blind man named Höichi, who was famed for his skill in recitation and in playing upon the *biwa*. From childhood he had been trained to recite and to play; and while yet a lad, he had surpassed his teachers. As a professional *biwa-höshi*/aéshi he became famous chiefly by his recitations of the history of the Heiké and the Genji; and it is said that when he sang the song of the battle of Dan-no-ura 'even the goblins [*kijin*] could not refrain from tears'.

At the outset of his career, Höichi was very poor; but he found a good friend to help him. The priest of the Amidaji was fond of poetry and music; and he often invited Höichi to the temple, to play and recite. Afterwards, being much impressed by the wonderful skill of the lad, the priest proposed that Höichi should make the temple his home; and this offer was gratefully accepted. Höichi was given a room in the temple-building; and, in return for food and lodging, he was required only to gratify the priest with a musical performance on certain evenings, when otherwise disengaged.

One summer night the priest was called away to perform a Buddhist service at the house of a dead parishioner; and he went there with his acolyte, leaving Höichi alone in the temple. It was a hot night; and the blind man sought to cool himself on the verandah before his sleeping-room. The verandah overlooked a small garden in the rear of the Amidaji. There Höichi waited for the priest's return, and tried to relieve his solitude by practising upon his *biwa*. Midnight passed; and the priest did not appear. But the atmosphere was still too warm for comfort within doors; and Hōichi remained outside. At last he heard steps approaching from the back gate. Somebody crossed the garden, advanced to the verandah, and halted directly in front of him—but it was not the priest. A deep voice called the blind man's name—abruptly and unceremoniously, in the manner of a Samurai summoning an inferior—

'Hōichi!'

Hōichi was too startled for the moment to respond; and the voice called again, in a tone of harsh command—

'Hōichi!'

'*Hai!*' answered the blind man, frightened by the menace in the voice—'I am blind!—I cannot know who calls!'

'There is nothing to fear,' the stranger exclaimed, speaking more gently. 'I am stopping near this temple, and have been sent to you with a message. My present lord, a person of exceedingly high rank, is now staying in Akamagaséki, with many noble attendants. He wished to view the scene of the battle of Dan-no-ura; and today he visited that place. Having heard of your skill in reciting the story of the battle, he now desires to hear your performance: so you will take your *biwa* and come with me at once to the house where the august assembly is waiting.'

In those times, the order of a Samurai was not to be lightly disobeyed. Hōichi donned his sandals, took his *biwa*, and went away with the stranger, who guided him deftly but obliged him to walk very fast. The hand that guided was iron; and the clank of the warrior's stride proved him fully armed—probably some palace-guard on duty. Hōichi's first alarm was over: he began to imagine himself in good luck; for, remembering the retainer's assurance about a 'person of exceedingly high rank', he thought that the lord who wished to hear the recitation could not be less than a daimyo of the first class. Presently the Samurai halted; and Hōichi became aware that they had arrived at a large gateway; and he wondered, for he could not remember any large gate in that part of the town, except the main gate of the Amidaji. '*Kaimon!*' the samurai called—and there was a sound of unbarring; and the twain passed on. They traversed a space of garden, and halted again before an entrance; and the retainer cried in a loud voice, 'Within there! I have brought Hōichi.' Then came the sounds of feet hurrying, and screens sliding, and rain-doors opening, and voices of women. By the language of the women Hōichi knew them to be domestics in some noble household; but he could not imagine to what place he had been conducted. Little time was allowed him for conjecture. After he had been helped to mount several stone steps, upon the last of which he was told to leave his sandals, a woman's hand guided him along interminable reaches of polished planking and round pillared angles, too many to remember, and over amazing widths of matted floor, into the middle of some vast apartment. There he thought that many great people were assembled: the sound of the rustling of silk was like the sound of leaves in a forest. He heard also a great humming of voices—talking in undertones; and the speech was the speech of courts.

Hōichi was told to put himself at ease, and he found a kneeling-cushion ready for him. After having taken his place upon it, and tuned his instrument, the voice of a woman—whom he divined to be the *Rōjo*, or matron in charge of the female service—addressed him, saying—

'It is now required that the history of the Hōichi be recited, to the accompaniment of the *biwa*.'

Now the entire recital would have required a time of many nights; therefore Hōichi ventured a question—

'As the whole of the story is not soon told, what portion

is it augustly desired that I now recite?'

The woman's voice made the answer—

'Recite the story of the battle at Dan-no-ura—for the pity of it is the most deep.'

Then Hōichi lifted his voice, and chanted the chant of the fight on the bitter sea, wonderfully making his *biwa* sound like the straining of oars and the rushing of ships, the whirr and the hissing of arrows, the shouting and trampling of men, the crashing of steel upon helmets, the plunging of the slain in the flood. And to the left and right of him, in the pauses of his playing, he could hear voices murmuring praise: 'How marvellous an artist!'—'Never in our own province was playing heard like this!'—'Not in all the empire is there another singer like Hōichi!' Then fresh courage came to him, and he played and sang yet better than before; and a hush of wonder deepened about him. But when at last he came to tell the fate of the fair and the helpless, the piteous perishing of the women and children, and the death-leap of Nii-no-Ania, with the imperial infant in her arms, all the listeners uttered together one long, long shuddering cry of anguish; and thereafter they wept and wailed so loudly and so wildly that the blind man was frightened by the violence of the grief that he had made. For much time the sobbing and the wailing continued. But gradually the sounds of lamentation died away; and again, in the great stillness that followed, Hōichi heard the voice of the woman whom he supposed to be the *Rōjo*.

She said—

'Although we had been assured that you were a very skilful player upon the *biwa*, and without an equal in recitative, we did not know that anyone could be so skilful as you have proved yourself tonight. Our lord has been pleased to say that he intends to bestow upon you a fitting reward. But he desires that you shall perform before him once every night for the next six nights—after which time he will probably make his august return journey. Tomorrow night, therefore, you are to come here at the same hour. The retainer who tonight conducted you will be sent for you. There is another matter about which I have been ordered to inform you. It is required that you shall speak to no one of your visits here, during the time of our lords' august sojourn at Akamagaséki. As he is travelling incognito, he commands that no mention of these things be made. You are now free to go back to your temple.'

After Hōichi had duly expressed his thanks, a woman's hand conducted him to the entrance of the house, where the same retainer, who had before guided him, was waiting to take him home. The retainer led him to the verandah at the rear of the temple, and there bade him farewell.

It was almost dawn when Hōichi returned; but his absence from the temple had not been observed, as the priest, coming back at a very late hour, had supposed him asleep. During the day Hōichi was able to take some rest; and he said nothing about his strange adventure. In the middle of the following night, the samurai again came for him, and led him to the august assembly, where he gave another recitation with the same success that had attended his previous performance. But during this second visit his absence from the temple was accidentally discovered; and after his return in the morning, he was summoned to the presence of the priest, who said to him in a tone of kindly reproach—

'We have been very anxious about you, friend Hōichi. To go out, blind and alone, at so late an hour, is dangerous. Why did you go without telling us? I could have ordered a servant to accompany you. And where have you been?'

Hōichi answered, evasively—

'Pardon me, kind friend! I had to attend to some private business; and I could not arrange the matter at any other hour.'

The priest was surprised, rather than pained, by Höichi's reticence; he felt it to be unnatural, and suspected something wrong. He feared that the blind lad had been bewitched or deluded by some evil spirits. He did not ask any more questions; but he privately instructed the men-servants of the temple to keep watch upon Höichi's movements, and to follow him in case he should again leave the temple after dark.

On the very next night, Höichi was seen to leave the temple; and the servants immediately lighted their lanterns, and followed him. But it was a rainy night, and very dark; and before the temple-folks could get to the roadway Höichi had disappeared. Evidently he had walked very fast—a strange thing, considering his blindness; for the road was in a bad condition. The men hurried through the streets, making inquiries at every house which Höichi was accustomed to visit; but nobody could give them any news of him. At last, as they were returning to the temple by way of the shore, they were startled by the sound of a *biwa*, furiously played, in the cemetery of the Amidaji. Except for some ghostly fires—such as usually flitted there on dark nights—all was blackness in that direction. But the men at once hastened to the cemetery; and there, by the help of their lanterns, they discovered Höichi—sitting alone in the rain before the memorial tomb of Antuko Tenno, making his *biwa* resound, and loudly chanting the chant of the battle of Dan-no-ura. And behind him, and about him, and everywhere above the tombs, the fires of the dead were burning, like candles. Never before had so great a host of *Oni-bi* appeared in the sight of mortal man…

'Höichi San!—Höichi San!' the servants cried. 'You are bewitched!… Höichi San!'

But the blind man did not seem to hear. Strenuously he made his *biwa* rattle and ring and clang; more wildly he chanted the chant of the battle of Dan-no-ura. They caught hold of him and shouted into his ear—

'Hōichi San!—Hōichi San!—come home with us at once!'

Reprovingly he spoke to them—

'To interrupt me in such a manner, before this august assembly, will not be tolerated.'

Whereat, in spite of the weirdness of the thing, the servants could not help laughing. Sure that he had been bewitched, they now seized him, and pulled him up on his feet, and by force hurried him back to the temple, where he was immediately relieved of his wet clothes, by order of the priest, and reclad, and made to eat and drink. Then the priest insisted upon a full explanation of his friend's astonishing behaviour.

Hōichi long hesitated to speak. But at last, finding that his conduct had really alarmed and angered the good priest, he decided to abandon his reserve; and he related everything that had happened from the time of the first visit of the samurai.

The priest said—

'Hōichi, my poor friend, you are now in great danger! How unfortunate that you did not tell me all this before! Your wonderful skill in music has indeed brought you strange trouble. By this time you must be aware that you have not been visiting any house whatever, but have been passing your nights in the cemetery, among the tombs of the Heiké; and it was before the memorial-tomb of Antoku Tenno that our people tonight found you, sitting in the rain. All that you have been imagining was illusion—except the calling of the dead. By once obeying them, you have put yourself in their power. If you obey them again, after what has already occurred, they will tear you to pieces. But they would have destroyed you, sooner or later, in any event. Now I shall not be able to remain with you tonight: I am called away to perform another service. But, before I go, it will be necessary to protect your body by writing holy texts upon it.'

Before sundown the priest and his acolyte stripped Hōichi: then, with their writing-brushes, they traced upon his breast and back, head and face and neck, limbs and hands and feet even upon the soles of his feet, and upon all parts of his body—the text of the holy sûtra called *Hannya-Shin-Kyō*. When this had been done, the priest instructed Hōichi, saying—

'Tonight, as soon as I go away, you must seat yourself on the verandah, and wait. You will be called. But whatever may happen, do not answer, and do not move. Say nothing, and sit still—as if meditating. If you stir, or make any noise, you will be torn asunder. Do not get frightened; and do not think of calling for help—because no help could save you. If you do exactly as I tell you, the danger will pass, and you will have nothing more to fear.'

After dark, the priest and the acolyte went away; and Hōichi sat himself on the verandah, according to the instructions given him. He laid his *biwa* on the planking beside him, and, assuming the attitude of meditation, remained quite still—taking care not to cough, or to breathe audibly. For hours he stayed thus.

Then, from the roadway, he heard the steps coming. They passed the gate, crossed the garden, approached the verandah, stopped directly in front of him.

'Hōichi!' the deep voice called. But the blind man held his breath, and sat motionless.

'Hōichi!' grimly called the voice a second time. Then a third time, savagely—

'Hōichi!'

Hōichi remained as still as a stone, and the voice grumbled—

'No answer!—that won't do... Must see where the fellow is.'

There was a noise of heavy feet mounting upon the verandah. The feet approached deliberately, and halted beside him. Then, for long minutes, during which Höichi felt his whole body shake to the beating of his heart, there was dead silence.

At last the gruff voice muttered close to him—

'Here is the *biwa*; but of its player I see—only two ears!... So that explains why he did not answer: he had no mouth to answer with—there is nothing left of him but his ears... Now to my lord those ears I will take in proof that the august commands have been obeyed, so far as was possible.'

At that instant Höichi felt his ears gripped by fingers of iron, and torn off! Great as the pain was, he gave no cry. The heavy footfalls receded along the verandah, descended into the garden, passed out to the roadway and ceased. From either side of his head, the blind man felt a thick, warm liquid trickling; but he dared not lift his hands.

Before sunrise the priest came back. He hastened at once to the verandah in the rear, stepped and slipped upon something clammy, and uttered a cry of horror, for he saw, by the light of his lantern, that the clamminess was blood. But he perceived Höichi sitting there, in the attitude of meditation—with the blood still oozing from his wounds.

'My poor Höichi!' cried the startled priest. 'What is this? You have been hurt?'

At the sound of his friend's voice, the blind man felt safe. He burst out sobbing, and tearfully told his adventure of the night.

'Poor, poor Höichi!' the priest exclaimed. 'All my fault! My very grievous fault! Everywhere upon your body the holy texts had been written—except upon your ears! I trusted my acolyte to do that part of the work; and it was very, very wrong of me not to have made sure that he had done it!... Well, the matter cannot now be helped; we can only try to heal your wounds as soon as possible. Cheer up, friend! The danger is now well over. You will never again be troubled by those visitors.'

With the aid of a good doctor, Hōichi soon recovered from his injuries. The story of his strange adventure spread far and wide, and soon made him famous. Many noble persons went to Akamagaséki to hear him recite; and large presents of money were given to him, so that he became a wealthy man. But from the time of his adventure, he was known only by the appellation of *Mimi-nashi-Hōichi:* 'Hōichi-the-Earless'.

THE THING IN THE UPPER ROOM

Arthur Morrison

A shadow hung ever over the door, which stood black in the depth of its arched recess, like an unfathomable eye under a frowning brow. The landing was wide and panelled, and a heavy rail, supported by a carved balustrade, stretched away in alternate slopes and levels down the dark staircase, past other doors, and so to the courtyard and the street. The other doors were dark also; but it was with a difference. That top landing was lightest of all, because of the skylight; and perhaps it was largely by reason of contrast that its one doorway gloomed so black and forbidding. The doors below opened and shut, slammed, stood ajar. Men and women passed in and out, with talk and human sounds—sometimes even with laughter or a snatch of song; but the door on the top landing remained shut and silent through weeks and months. For, in truth, the logement had an ill name, and had been untenanted for years. Long even before the last tenant had occupied it, the room had been regarded with fear and aversion, and the end of that last tenant had in no way lightened the gloom that hung about the place.

The house was so old that its weather-washed face may well have looked down on the bloodshed of St. Bartholomew's, and the haunted room may even have earned its ill name on that same day of death. But Paris is a city of cruel history, and since the old mansion rose proud and new, the hotel of some powerful noble, almost any year of the centuries might have seen the blot fall on that upper room that had left it a place of loathing and shadows. The occasion was long forgotten, but the fact remained; whether or not some horror of the ancient régime or some enormity of the terror was enacted in that room was no longer to be discovered; but nobody would live there, not stay beyond that gloomy door one second longer than he could help. It might be supposed that the fate of the solitary tenant within living memory had something to do with the matter—and, indeed, his end was sinister enough; but 'long before his time the room had stood shunned and empty. He, greatly daring, had taken no more heed of the common terror of the room than to use it to his advantage in abating the rent; and he had shot himself a little later, while the police were beating at his door to arrest him on a charge of murder. As I have said, his fate may have added to the general aversion from the place, though it had in no way originated it; and now ten years had passed, and more, since his few articles of furniture had been carried away and sold; and nothing had been carried in to replace them.

When one is twenty-five, healthy, hungry and poor, one is less likely to be frightened from a cheap lodging by mere headshakings than might be expected in other circumstances. Attwater was twenty-five, commonly healthy, often hungry, and always poor. He came to live in Paris because, from his remembrance of his student days, he believed he could live cheaper there than in London; while it was quite certain that he would not sell fewer pictures, since he had never yet sold one.

It was the concierge of a neighbouring house who showed

Attwater the room. The house of the room itself maintained no such functionary, though its main door stood open day and night. The man said little, but his surprise at Attwater's application was plain to see. Monsieur was English? Yes. The logement was convenient, though high, and probably now a little dirty, since it had not been occupied recently. Plainly, the man felt it to be no business of his to enlighten an unsuspecting foreigner as to the reputation of the place; and if he could let it there would be some small gratification from the landlord, though, at such a rent, of course a very small one indeed.

But Attwater was better informed than the concierge supposed. He had heard the tale of the haunted room, vaguely and incoherently, it is true, from the little old engraver of watches on the floor below, by whom he had been directed to the concierge. The old man had been voluble and friendly, and reported that the room had a good light, facing north-east—indeed, a much better light than he, engraver of watches, enjoyed on the floor below. So much so that, considering this advantage and the much lower rent, he himself would have taken the room long ago, except—well, except for other things. Monsieur was a stranger, and perhaps had no fear to inhabit a haunted chamber; but that was its reputation, as everybody in the quarter knew; it would be a misfortune, however, to a stranger to take the room without suspicion, and to undergo unexpected experiences. Here, however, the old man checked himself, possibly reflecting that too much information to inquirers after the upper room might offend his landlord. He hinted as much, in fact, hoping that his friendly warning would not be allowed to travel farther. As to the precise nature of the disagreeable manifestations in the room, who could say? Perhaps there were really none at all. People said this and that. Certainly, the place had been untenanted for many years, and he would not like to stay in it himself. But it might be the good fortune of monsieur to break the spell, and if monsieur was resolved to defy the revenant, he wished monsieur the highest success and happiness.

So much for the engraver of watches; and now the concierge of the neighbouring house led the way up the stately old panelled staircase, swinging his keys in his hand, and halted at last before the dark door in the frowning recess. He turned the key with some difficulty, pushed open the door, and stood back with an action of something not wholly deference, to allow Attwater to enter first.

A sort of small lobby had been partitioned off at some time, though except for this the logement was of one large room only. There was something unpleasant in the air of the place—not a smell, when one came to analyse one's sensations, though at first it might seem so. Attwater walked across to the wide window and threw it open. The chimneys and roofs of many houses of all ages straggled before him, and out of the welter rose the twin towers of St. Sulpice, scarred and grim.

Air the room as one might, it was unpleasant; a sickly, even a cowed, feeling, invaded one through all the senses—or perhaps through none of them. The feeling was there, though it was not easy to say by what channel it penetrated. Attwater was resolved to admit none but a common-sense explanation, and blamed the long closing of door and window; and the concierge, standing uneasily near the door, agreed that that must be it. For a moment Attwater wavered, despite himself. But the rent was very low, and, low as it was, he could not afford a sou more. The light was good, though it was not a top-light, and the place was big enough for his simple requirements. Attwater reflected that he should despise himself ever after if he shrank from the opportunity; it would be one of those secret humiliations that will rise again and again in a man's memory, and make him blush in solitude. He told the concierge to leave door and window wide open for the rest of the day, and he clinched the bargain.

It was with something of amused bravado that he reported to his few friends in Paris his acquisition of a haunted room; for, once out of the place, he readily convinced himself that his disgust and dislike while in the room were the result of imagination and nothing more. Certainly, there was no rational reason to account for the unpleasantness; consequently, what could it be but a matter of fancy? He resolved to face the matter from the beginning, and clear his mind from any foolish prejudices that the hints of the old engraver might have inspired, by forcing himself through whatever adventures he might encounter. In fact, as he walked the streets about his business, and arranged for the purchase and delivery of the few simple articles of furniture that would be necessary, his enterprise assumed the guise of a pleasing adventure. He remembered that he had made an attempt, only a year or two ago, to spend a night in a house reputed haunted in England, but had failed to find the landlord. Here was the adventure to hand, with promise of a tale to tell in future times; and a welcome idea struck him that he might look out the ancient history of the room, and work the whole thing into a magazine article, which would bring a little money.

So simple were his needs that by the afternoon of the day following his first examination of the room it was ready for use. He took his bag from the cheap hotel in a little street of Montparnasse, where he had been lodging, and carried it to his new home. The key was now in his pocket, and for the first time he entered the place alone. The window remained wide open; but it was still there—that depressing, choking something that entered the consciousness he knew not by what gate. Again he accused his fancy. He stamped and whistled, and set about unpacking a few canvases and a case of old oriental weapons that were part of his professional properties. But he could give no proper attention to the work, and detected himself more than once yielding to a childish impulse to look over his shoulder. He laughed at himself—with some effort—and sat determinedly to smoke a pipe, and grow used to his surroundings. But presently he found himself pushing his chair farther and farther back, till it touched the wall. He would take the whole room into view, he said to himself in excuse, and stare it out of countenance. So he sat and smoked, and as he sat his eye fell on a Malay dagger that lay on the table between him and the window. It was a murderous, twisted thing, and its pommel was fashioned into the semblance of a bird's head, with curved beak and an eye of some dull red stone. He found himself gazing on this red eye with an odd, mindless fascination. The dagger in its wicked curves seemed now a creature of some outlandish fantasy—a snake with a beaked head, a thing of nightmare, in some new way dominant, overruling the centre of his perceptions. The rest of the room grew dim, but the red stone glowed with a fuller light; nothing more was present to his consciousness, Then, with a sudden clang, the heavy bell of St. Sulpice aroused him, and he started up in some surprise.

There lay the dagger on the table, strange and murderous enough, but merely as he had always known it. He observed with more surprise, however, that his chair, which had been back against the wall, was now some six feet forward, close by the table; clearly, he must have drawn it forward in his abstraction, towards the dagger on which his eyes had been fixed... The great bell of St. Sulpice went clanging on, repeating its monotonous call to the Angelus.

He was cold, almost shivering. He flung the dagger into a

drawer, and turned to go out. He saw by his watch that it was later than he had supposed; his fit of abstraction must have lasted some time. Perhaps he had even been dozing.

He went slowly downstairs and out into the streets. As he went he grew more and more ashamed of himself, for he had to confess that in some inexplicable way he feared that room. He had seen nothing, heard nothing of the kind that one might have expected, or had heard of in any room reputed haunted; he could not help thinking that it would have been some sort of relief if he had. But there was an all-pervading, overpowering sense of another Presence—something abhorrent, not human, something almost physically nauseous. Withal it was something more than presence; it was power, domination—so he seemed to remember it. And yet the remembrance grew weaker as he walked in the gathering dusk; he thought of a story he had once read of a haunted house wherein it was shown that the house actually was haunted—by the spirit of fear, and nothing else. That, he persuaded himself, was the case with his room; he felt angry at the growing conviction that he had allowed himself to be overborne by fancy—by the spirit of fear.

He returned that night with the resolve to allow himself no foolish indulgence. He had heard nothing and had seen nothing; when something palpable to the senses occurred, it would be time enough to deal with it. He took off his clothes and got into bed deliberately, leaving candle and matches at hand in case of need. He had expected to find some difficulty in sleeping, or at least some delay, but he was scarce well in bed ere he fell into a heavy sleep.

Dazzling sunlight through the window woke him in the morning, and he sat up, staring sleepily about him. He must have slept like a log. But he had been dreaming; the dreams were horrible. His head ached beyond anything he had experienced before, and he was far more tired than when he went to bed. He sank back on the pillow, but the mere contact made his head ring with pain. He got out of bed, and found himself staggering; it was all as though he had been drunk—unspeakably drunk with bad liquor. His dreams—they had been horrid dreams; he could remember that they had been bad; but what they actually were was now gone from him entirely. He rubbed his eyes and stared amazedly down at the table: where the crooked dagger lay, with its bird's head and red stone eye. It lay just as it had lain when he sat gazing at it yesterday, and yet he would have sworn that he had flung that same dagger into a drawer. Perhaps he had dreamed it; at any rate, he put the thing carefully into the drawer now; and, still with his ringing headache, dressed himself and went out.

As he reached the next landing the old engraver greeted him from his door with an inquiring good-day. 'Monsieur has not slept well, I fear?'

In some doubt, Attwater protested that he had slept quite soundly, 'And as yet I have neither seen nor heard anything of the ghost,' he added.

'Nothing?' replied the old man, with a lift of the eyebrows, 'nothing at all? It is fortunate. It seemed to me, here below, that monsieur was moving about very restlessly in the night; but no doubt I was mistaken. No doubt, also, I may felicitate monsieur on breaking the evil tradition. We shall hear no more of it; monsieur has the good fortune of a brave heart.'

He smiled and bowed pleasantly, but it was with something of a puzzled look that his eyes followed Attwater descending the staircase.

Attwater took his coffee and roll after an hour's walk, and fell asleep in his seat. Not for long, however, and presently he rose and left the cafe. He felt better, though still unaccountably fatigued. He caught sight of his face in a mirror beside a shop window, and saw an improvement since he had looked in his own glass. That indeed had brought him a shock. Worn and drawn beyond what might have been expected of so bad a night, there was even something more. What was it? How should it remind him of that old legend—was it Japanese?—which he had tried to recollect when he had wondered confusedly at the haggard apparition that confronted him? Some tale of a demon-possessed person who in any mirror, saw never his own face, but the face of the demon.

Work he felt to be impossible, and he spent the day on garden seats, at café tables, and for a while in the Luxembourg. And in the evening he met an English friend, who took him by the shoulders and looked into his eyes, shook him, and declared that he had been overworking, and needed, above all things, a good dinner, which he should have instantly. 'You'll dine with me,' he said, 'at La Perouse, and we'll get a cab to take us there. I'm hungry.'

As they stood and looked for a passing cab a man ran shouting with newspapers. 'We'll have a cab,' Attwater's friend repeated, 'and we'll take the new murder with us for conversation's sake. Hi! *Journal!*'

He bought a paper, and followed Attwater into the cab. 'I've a strong idea I knew the poor old boy by sight,' he said. 'I believe he'd seen better days.'

'Who?'

'The old man who was murdered in the Rue Broca last night. The description fits exactly. He used to hang about the cafés and run messages. It isn't easy to read in this cab; but there's probably nothing fresh in this edition. They haven't caught the murderer, anyhow.'

Attwater took the paper, and struggled to read it in the

changing light. A poor old man had been found dead on the footpath of the Rue Broca, torn with a score of stabs. He had been identified—an old man not known to have a friend in the world; also, because he was so old and so poor, probably not an enemy. There was no robbery; the few sous the old man possessed remained in his pocket. He must have been attacked on his way home in the early hours of the morning, possibly by a homicidal maniac, and stabbed again and again with inconceivable fury. No arrest had been made.

Attwater pushed the paper away: 'Pah!' he said; 'I don't like it. I'm a bit off colour and I was dreaming horribly all last night; thought why this should remind me of it I can't guess. But it's no cure for the blues, this!'

'No,' replied his friend heartily. 'We'll get that upstairs, for here we are, on the quay. A bottle of the best Burgundy on the list and the best dinner they can do—that's your physic. Come!'

It was a good prescription, indeed. Attwater's friend was cheerful and assiduous, and nothing could have bettered the dinner. Attwater found himself reflecting that indulgence in the blues was a poor pastime, with no better excuse than a bad night's rest. And last night's dinner in comparison with this! Well, it was enough to have spoiled his sleep, that one franc-fifty dinner.

Attwater left La Perouse as gay as his friend. They had sat late, and now there was nothing to do but cross the water and walk a little in the boulevards. This they did, and finished the evening at a café table with half a dozen acquaintances.

Attwater walked home with a light step, feeling less drowsy than at any time during the day. He was well enough. He felt he should soon get used to the room. He had been a little too much alone lately, and that had got on his nerves. It was simply stupid.

Again he slept quickly and heavily—and dreamed. But he had an awakening of another sort. No bright sun blazed in at the open window to lift his heavy lids, and no morning bell from St. Sulpice opened his ears to the cheerful noise of the city. He awoke gasping and staring in the dark, rolling face-downward on the floor, catching his breath in agonized sobs; while through the window from the streets came a clamour of hoarse cries: cries of pursuit and the noise of running men: a shouting and clatter wherein here and there a voice was clear among the rest—*Al'assassin! Arrêtez!'*

He dragged himself to his feet in the dark, gasping still. What was this—all this? Again a dream? His legs trembled under him, and he sweated with fear. He made for the window, panting and feeble; and then, as he supported himself by the sill, he realized wonderingly that he was fully dressed—that he wore even his hat. The running crowd straggled through the outer street and away, the shouts growing fainter. What had wakened him? Why had he dressed? He remembered his matches, and turned to grope for them; but something was already in his hand—something wet, sticky. He dropped it on the table, and even as he struck the light, before he saw it, he knew. The match sputtered and flared, and there on the table lay the crooked dagger, smeared and dripping and horrible.

Blood was on his hands—the match stuck in his fingers. Caught at the heart by the first grip of an awful surmise, he hooked up and saw in the mirror before him, in the last flare of the match, the face of the Thing in the room.